INAUTHENTICITY

by Robert Rahula

ALSO BY ROBERT RAHULA

NOVELS:
Messieurs
Panamaniac
Island of Misfits
Day Another Paradise In
One Last Fling
Bathhouse Stories
Conversation in a Belgian Bar
All the Yage in Reno
Exigent Circumstances
Uninvited Guest
A Modest Summation of Things
To Die in Toledo
The Treasure of the Gran Ventura

SHORT STORIES:
Horror Stories for Children
Behind the Pearly Gates

POETRY:
Trigger Points
Dentro Del Corazón Bloqueada
Camino
Migration
I Sing the Body Politic
Wonderland
From Whose Bourn
Poemas Españoles
Expat Poems
Old Dogs New Poems

ANTHOLOGIES:
Half Life
The Essential Dan Landes
50 Years Down the Drain

INAUTHENTICITY

© 2024 by Robert Rahula

www.robertrahula.com

This is a work of fiction. Characters, organizations, businesses, products, locales, and events portrayed in this book either are products of the author's imagination or are used fictitiously.

Thanks to Red Dress Press, Liz, Chris, and Em for editing, proofreading, and artwork.

ISBN 979-8-9897238-0-5

Alma-gator Press

Barcelona • Madrid • La Chorrera

CHAPTER ONE

Everyone has a lucky number. In fact, most people who have one lucky number usually have several. Ricardo was no exception. He had his favorite numbers, and he bet them each week in the Panamanian lottery. He liked playing the Panamanian lottery, which was convenient because that was the only lottery that was available in the country in which he lived—which was Panama—in the town of Villa Rosario, to be exact. There was a different lottery drawing every evening, but Ricardo only played on Tuesdays. That's the thing about people with lucky numbers—they are often rather superstitious. Tuesday was Ricardo's lucky day, so he would always bet ten dollars on his lucky numbers on his lucky day. He did not stand in line at the lottery booth like most Panamanians. No, no. He was more civilized, i.e., more lazy. He played online. He would fire up his computer every Tuesday morning over coffee, and place his bet, always playing his same lucky numbers.

The Tuesday lottery drawing was, of course, on Tuesday night. It was broadcast on Panamanian TV with a lot of hoopla and fanfare and falling confetti. But Ricardo did not watch that show. If he won any money—which, to be honest, was quite rare—the lottery system would notify him by email.

But, on this particular Tuesday evening, Ricardo actually won. He didn't match all of the numbers, but he matched enough to win four hundred dollars. Not a lot of money to a gringo, but still, nothing to sneeze at. Certainly, it was something to celebrate, and the best way to celebrate an unexpected windfall is to take your friends out to dinner. And so it was that Ricardo organized a dinner party for the following Saturday night. He called his best friend, Dan Landes, and asked him who he should invite. Of course, Dan suggested his friend, don Fernando, the police chief of Villa Rosario. Ricardo readily agreed, thinking that there might be drinking at the dinner, and it would be very helpful to have the chief of police with them in case there were any problems. And Dan also suggested don Fernando's nephew, Jorge Manuel, who was the police chief of the neighboring city of La Chorrera. Ricardo also agreed to that, because as everyone knows, two police chiefs are better than one. Then Ricardo suggested that the dinner be held at the Los Cuñados restaurant in La Chorrera. Not only was Los Cuñados Ricardo's favorite restaurant, but it was owned by his long-time friend Miguel, and Ricardo always liked to throw any business Miguel's way that he could.

And so it was that the four men, Ricardo, Dan, don Fernando, and Jorge Manuel ended up sitting together at a table in the Los Cuñados restaurant on this particular Saturday night. And, as fate would have it, Dan was seated next to Jorge Manuel.

Fate is an interesting concept, don't you think? We apply it to everything significant in our lives, both good and bad. If anything happens that creates a chain of events, we always say, "as fate would have it", as if fate was sitting around thinking about us and deciding whether to have it or not to have it. Ricardo was a big believer in fate, but Dan was just the opposite. Dan believed that the only way things happened was by hard work and mental focus. But of course, Dan was a retired police detective from the LA police force, so naturally he would feel that way. His whole adult life's experience was being surrounded by crime, criminals, random violent events, and horrible outcomes. The only way crimes were solved—in Dan's experience—was by hard detective work that focused on evidence. Ricardo, on the other hand, was a writer, and a successful one. He didn't know why his books sold, but they did, and he made a living at it. To Ricardo, good things just happened out of the blue. So, for him, fate was an active force in his life, sitting somewhere up in the clouds making things happen. Two best friends with completely opposite experiences and completely opposite frames of reference... it's hard to say who was right. Maybe life is a combination of both: random horrible events and serendipitous connections with good results.

But I digress. I'm just telling you what happened. Ricardo won four hundred dollars in the lottery, and so he invited his three friends to a free dinner, and all four men ended up in Los Cuñados restaurant on that particular Saturday night, and Dan ended up sitting next to Jorge Manuel.

And because Dan was a retired detective and Jorge Manuel was a police chief, they ended up talking about crime, and... as fate would have it... they were talking about a particular odd autopsy that had happened earlier that week in La Chorrera.

"It was very strange, señor Landes," Jorge Manuel was saying to Dan, "because, on the surface, it just appeared that another gringo had had a heart attack and died. He was at his desk, and he simply kneeled over and died. The coroner said it was a heart attack, but then we asked his personal doctor, and he said that the victim had no history of heart problems. And that bothered me. Normally, we don't do autopsies when gringos die, but something didn't seem right. I had—what do you call it?—a hunch? I had a hunch something was wrong. So, I ordered an autopsy."

"Who was the guy?" Dan asked. "I mean, what was his name?"

"Isaiah Leaf," said Jorge Manuel.

"Leaf?" asked Dan, "like a leaf on a plant?"

"Yes."

"Odd name," said Dan, "but I've never heard of him. Had he lived in La Chorrera a long time?"

"About a year and a half," said Jorge Manuel. "He was one of those—how do you say?—digital nomads. He had a digital nomad visa and he worked from his home."

"Well, my experience with hunches," Dan said, "is that there is usually something very rational behind them, some small detail that seems odd. So let me ask you: what bothered you about this man's death that made you order an autopsy?"

Jorge Manuel thought for a minute and then said, "Well, it was two things. First, as I mentioned, his personal physician told me that the man had no history of heart problems. And second, his wife didn't seem distraught. I mean, she was upset; she was crying; but she was not overwhelmed with grief. At first, I thought it was the difference in cultures, you know. In my experience, gringos don't have any emotions—not like our people. I would expect a Panamanian woman to be inconsolable if her husband had just died, but I don't expect that from a gringo's wife."

Dan nodded his head. He thought there was truth in Jorge Manuel's words.

"But still, it bothered you?" Dan asked. "The fact that this woman wasn't grieving?"

"It bothered me," agreed Jorge Manuel.

"Well, I think hunches are important," Dan said, "and if it had been me, I would have ordered an autopsy too. I think you did the right thing."

Jorge Manuel smiled. He was a young man to be a police chief, and Dan, who was much older and more experienced, always noticed that Jorge Manuel smiled when Dan complimented his work.

"What did the autopsy show?" Dan asked.

"Well, he did die of a heart attack," admitted Jorge Manuel. "I have to say, I was a bit disappointed. Now my department will have to bear the cost of the autopsy. The coroner listed the cause of death as a health-related heart attack. The only thing that I didn't understand is that there was an unusual substance in his blood. The coroner didn't know what it was, but he didn't think it was important."

"What was it?" Dan asked.

"I cannot pronounce it," Jorge Manuel said, as he reached into his pocket, but I brought the autopsy report with me.

Jorge Manuel pulled a two-page report that had been carefully folded into a small square from his shirt pocket. He unfolded the paper and searched through the typed pages until he found what he was looking for.

"It was te-tra-hy-droz-oline," he said, pronouncing it slowly, syllable by syllable.

Dan put his fork down and stared at Jorge Manuel.

"Tetrahydrozoline? That's Visine, Jorge," Dan said.

"What is Visine, señor?" Jorge Manuel asked.

"Eye drops, Jorge, eye drops. You can buy Visine in the drug stores in the States; the pharmacies probably carry it here. It's a small bottle of liquid, and you put drops of it in your eyes when your eyes are red or irritated. Can I see that report?"

Jorge Manuel handed Dan the pages. Dan scanned the report quickly, reading the key points out loud to himself. "Fifty-two-year-old, well-developed, well-nourished white male... blah blah... no external indications of trauma... blah blah blah... heart 380 grams, normal size and shape... minimal atherosclerosis... no measurable plaque... okay, where's the cause of death? Oh, here we go... due to lack of structural cardiac abnormalities, the cause of death is presumed atrioventricular block caused by sudden onset of arrhythmia..."

Dan went to the second page and scanned it. "Okay, stomach was empty, he hadn't eaten anything... where's the bloodwork? Okay, here it is... toxicology test was positive for marijuana—well, that's common—and tetrahydrozoline. Interesting."

Dan frowned. Jorge Manuel saw this as his opportunity to ask, "So this drug goes from your eyes into your blood?"

"Ah, no, Jorge," Dan said. "The only way it gets into your blood is if you drink it. But you can't drink it—it's poisonous.

It can cause a heart attack. Don't you see? Tetrahydrozoline is a clear liquid; it has no taste or odor. If someone put it into this man's drink or food, and if he consumed enough of it, he would have a heart attack. Your hunch was correct. This man may have been murdered."

Jorge Manuel's eyes widened. Everyone at the table was quiet now, as they had all heard the M word. Dan looked at the report again.

"The blood test didn't show how much tetrahydrozoline was in this man's blood... oh, I see, they just used a Conklin Toxicology test." He looked up at Jorge Manuel and explained, "That's a cheap test that just gives you a yes or no answer as to the presence of drugs. Where's the man's body now? I would recommend taking another blood sample and sending it to a lab to determine how much tetrahydrozoline was in his system."

Jorge Manuel frowned and shook his head. "I cannot do that, señor. Once the coroner signed off on the death certificate, we released the body to his wife, and she had it cremated."

"Ahh," said Dan. "How convenient."

Don Fernando spoke up. "Who performed this autopsy, Koke?" he asked, addressing Jorge Manuel by his family nickname.

"We had to use Doctor Javier Hugo," Jorge Manuel said. "Our regular coroner was out of town."

"Ah," said don Fernando, and then, turning to Dan, he said, "That doctor does not work very hard. To be honest, he is lazy, although to be fair, he does not get much practice in doing autopsies in La Chorrera."

Dan nodded and handed the autopsy report back to Jorge Manuel.

"What would you recommend?" Jorge Manuel asked.

"Well," Dan said, I would recommend keeping the investigation open. Keep poking around and see what turns up."

Dan picked up his fork and began eating again.

Jorge Manuel looked confused. "What does this mean, 'poking around'? Is it like hitting people."

"No, no, Jorge," Dan said and smiled. "It means to keep investigating, keep asking questions, keep digging and see what you find. See if the pharmacies near where this man lived carry Visine or other eye drops that might contain tetrahydrozoline. See if the wife bought some eye drops recently. See if the man had a life insurance policy. See if the marriage had problems. Just keep... *poking around.*"

Jorge Manuel nodded and said, "Gracias, señor Dani. I will be poking around."

CHAPTER TWO

And Jorge Manuel did poke around. Or rather, he had his sergeant poke around. Sergeant Sotto had been on the La Chorrera police force longer than Jorge Manuel had been police chief. In fact, years ago, when don Fernando was orchestrating the appointment of his nephew as police chief, don Fernando made it a point to personally speak with Sergeant Sotto to ask for his support. Jorge Manuel was a young man, and don Fernando knew that Jorge Manuel would need the support of the older officers on the La Chorrera force if he was going to succeed as police chief. There is nothing so fatal to new authority as resentful employees, especially resentful older employees. So, don Fernando needed Sergeant Sotto's agreement to help his nephew succeed as the new police chief. There may have been some gifts involved, some quid pro quo that occurred at this meeting—I'm not saying. I'm just telling you what happened. Don Fernando wanted his nephew to be successful as the La Chorrera police chief, so he arranged a private personal meeting with Sergeant Sotto. And, as fate would have it, Jorge Manuel turned out to be a good police chief, popular with the rank and file.

And so it was that, following his conversation with Dan Landes at that dinner at the Los Cuñados restaurant, Jorge Manuel met with Sergeant Sotto and told him what Dan Landes had said about the tetrahydrozoline that had shown up in the autopsy, and what that might mean. Sergeant Sotto nodded his head. He did not personally know Dan Landes, but he did know that Dan Landes was don Fernando's close friend, and that was good enough for him. So, when Jorge

Manuel asked Sergeant Sotto to "poke around" and see what he could turn up regarding the deceased Isaiah Leaf, Sergeant Sotto agreed.

Sergeant Sotto was a natural-born "poker-arounder." He was a big man, but completely unassuming in his manner. He had a round, smooth face that was reassuring, but easy to forget. And most importantly, he spoke with a soft, friendly voice that lulled anyone he was interviewing into sharing more information than perhaps they wanted. His voice was so soft that you had to lean forward to hear him. That closeness of conversation seemed to inspire confidence and evoke trust from the person being questioned. Sergeant Sotto's voice was so disarming that his fellow officers would often joke that he could sweet talk a suspect into confessing. Another attribute of Sergeant Sotto's interviewing style is that he never took notes. He had long ago learned that everyone is suspicious when you write down what they say, so he had trained himself to have a perfect memory. He would return to his desk after interviewing someone and type up a verbatim transcript of what they had said.

And so it was that, a week later, Sergeant Sotto reported back to Jorge Manuel. Sergeant Sotto had spoken at length with Isaiah Leaf's wife, Melissa Leaf. He provided Jorge Manuel with a transcript of their conversation. Sergeant Sotto had also interviewed Mark Handel, who had been Isaiah Leaf's business partner. From these two interviews, Sergeant Sotto and Jorge Manuel pieced together a rather complicated picture of the late Isaiah Leaf.

Isaiah Leaf and his business partner Mark Handel had moved to La Chorrera from Los Angeles a year and a half ago. They both had obtained digital nomad visas—a new type of visa being touted by Panama's government to bring entrepreneurs, and their dollars, to Panama. The visa was only available to foreigners who made their living online. The government was historically very stingy with work visas. They didn't want foreigners moving to Panama and taking jobs away from locals. The government was sick of young (and not so young) gringos moving to Panama for the low cost of living and the good weather, and then supporting themselves by taking jobs as bartenders, real estate agents, masseuses, personal trainers, etc., jobs that Panamanians could do. Every normal job that a gringo took in Panama meant one less job for a local. But if a foreigner could demonstrate that he or she had an online business; that they worked exclusively online; that their business existed before they moved to Panama; that they weren't taking a job away from a Panamanian; and that they netted at least fifty thousand dollars a year from their online job, then the Panamanian government was very pleased to offer them a two-year, renewable, digital nomad visa... provided the foreigner opened up a Panamanian bank account and placed the proceeds of his or her digital business in that bank account. As far as the Panamanian government was concerned, the more self-supporting gringos who moved their internet headquarters to Panama, the better. They could generate as much money as they wanted online, as long as they supported the local economy in Panama by paying rent, buying food, paying for entertainment, etc. In fact, the Panamanian government was so enthusiastic about attracting digital nomads to Panama that they didn't really care what type of online business these nomads were operating, as long as it was profitable. The official government policy was to look the other way when it came to the nature of these various online enterprises. And thus it was that Panama began to attract some rather questionable online activities, like sports betting, bitcoin investing, or as in the case of Isaiah Leaf and Mark Handel, pornography.

Now, that might seem quite odd, Panama being a Catholic country and all. There were strict laws against human trafficking, and strict laws against the making of pornographic films in Panama. So how was it that Isaiah Leaf and Mark Handel (who were major players in the Los Angeles adult film business) were able to produce pornographic films in Panama? The answer was because Isaiah Leaf and Mark Handel didn't produce their pornographic films *inside* Panama. The only equipment that they used was one laptop computer. The actual production of the pornography happened inside giant computer servers that were located in Nevada.

As Sergeant Soto discovered in his interviews with Melissa Leaf and Mark Handel, the late Isaiah Leaf had been somewhat of a computer coding genius, a pioneer in the field of artificial intelligence, *and* a fanatic devotee of pornography. He had managed to do what so few people do in life: fuse his personal passion with his abilities. His passion—or rather, his addiction—was pornography; and his ability was computer programming. And thus it was that Isaiah Leaf had developed the first AI program that could create life-like pornography without using real people.

As a teenager, Isaiah Leaf had been fascinated by "porno cartoons." These were short X-rated cartoons that were shown between real adult pornography films in the adult theatres in downtown LA. These cartoons gave the projectionist time to change the reels of film for the next full-length actual porn movie. The cartoons were short and funny—an X-rated intermission of sorts.

Religious and conservative groups were always trying to outlaw pornography, of course. During Isaiah Leaf's first year studying computer programming at the University of California at Berkeley, a particular Supreme Court case caught his attention. Some religious group had sued a cartoon company for making porno cartoons, and the Supreme Court had dismissed the lawsuit on the grounds that no real people were being depicted in the cartoons, and thus the cartoons fell under the higher standards of protection granted to intellectual property, such as literature. As time went on, and reels of film were replaced first by video cassettes, and then by DVDs, and then by streaming services, the porno cartoons disappeared. But that little-known Supreme Court case had always stuck in Isaiah Leaf's mind. He realized that if he could make a realistic, life-like, explicit, adult film using only computer-generated imagery (or CGI,) then it would be exempt from the increasing legal restrictions on porn movies, not to mention the fact that it would eliminate the unnecessary cost of hiring real actors, cameramen, lighting directors and such. Isaiah Leaf realized that the profit margin could be huge, and so he quit the university during his second year and devoted the rest of his life to making completely digital, totally artificial, but totally realistic, graphic CGI pornography. His first efforts were stilted, jerky, barely plausible montages. But gradually, over the years, he got better at it. His big breakthrough came when he started to use AI language in programming the CGI images, where the programming would teach itself how to improve, would teach itself how to mimic images of real human intercourse and other sexual acts. He sold his first believable artificial porn movie to a San Francisco hedge fund for twenty thousand dollars. He then used that money to buy and install his own servers in Nevada, just outside of Reno. He spent the next few years cranking out straight porn, gay porn, trans porn, lesbian porn, and more. He and his business partner Mark Handel began making some serious money.

Mark Handel was a disbarred lawyer who Isaiah happened to meet just after he had sold his first porno film. Mark Handel had gotten disbarred because he had shown up drunk to court a few times too often. Drinking was Mark's one weakness. He was actually a very smart lawyer, but he was a bit of a drunk... and a bit of a womanizer... and a pornography enthusiast. Isaiah and Mark had formed an instant bond over their mutual love of pornography and their mutual hatred of any kind of government authority. It was Mark Handel who convinced Isaiah to incorporate Fig Leaf Cybernetics as a movie production company, and then to hide that corporation under layers and layers of offshore shell companies. Mark Handel's theory was that even if Isaiah's films were protected from criminal prosecution by that Supreme Court decision, why take any chances in connecting Isaiah to the films? "If they don't know who you are, they can't arrest you," Mark was fond of saying.

Melissa Leaf was the one who had come up with the name of the movie company. She thought it was a clever twist on Isaiah's last name. Melissa had been a young porn actress that Isaiah had met when he was just getting started in the movie business. He had originally hired her as a porn model to teach his AI program how human beings move during sex. He and Melissa would get naked, and Isaiah would cover both their bodies with dot electrodes, and then they would make love in every position that they could think of. Isaiah would feed the video and electrode information directly into his computer program, and then instruct the program to create different faces and bodies that followed the same movements.

Isaiah and Melissa would meet twice a week for months on end, just to record their sexual escapades. It was a purely business arrangement. But you know how sex is: it can undermine even the best of plans. Isaiah and Melissa fell in love, and so they married.

As the Fig Leaf Cybernetic films got better and more popular, they started drawing the attention of different federal organizations. But there was nothing they could do. Each film carried a clear disclaimer that no real people were used in the making of the film. Besides, thanks to Mark Handel's layering of shell company owners, there was nothing that connected Isaiah Leaf to the films. The only legal problems that Isaiah faced were protests from FUPA, the Federal Union of Porn Actors. There was a growing fear among all porn actors and actresses that CGI porn was going to put them out of work. This fear was real, because most of these actors and actresses had no real skills outside of fucking and sucking. FUPA started to organize rallies and protests outside of theatres showing Fig Leaf Cybernetic films. Both Mark and Isaiah were concerned that these protests would discourage theatres from showing his films. So they followed the course of action that all business leaders and politicians advocate in times of political unrest: they bribed their opponents. They donated hundreds of thousands of dollars to FUPA's union leadership under the guise of grants for education, STD testing programs, or promotional research. There was no specific quid pro quo to these grants, but Mark Handel designed each grant so that there were no financial controls, so the FUPA union leaders did what all leaders do when there are no financial controls: they pocketed the money. Union leaders may be a lot of things, but they are not dumb. They knew the money came from Fig Leaf Cybernetics; they knew there were no financial controls; they appreciated their new source of income; and they intuited that if they continued to protest Fig Leaf films, that the money would end. So, the protests quietly died away. Fig Leaf Cybernetics wrote off the bribes as charity donations; FUPA continued to advocate for their union members who worked in actual porn movies; and life was good.

Maybe it was the fact that things were going so well that bothered Isaiah. Melissa Leaf wasn't sure why Isaiah wanted to move to Panama. She told Sergeant Sotto that one day Isaiah simply announced that he was going to relocate the business and both their lives out of the US. Mark Handel told Sergeant Sotto the same thing, but Sergeant Sotto had the clear impression that neither of them were telling him everything they knew about the move. Of course, he didn't push the issue. He was just glad he had gotten so much information out of the two, especially from Mark Handel. Sergeant Sotto had spent several late nights with Mark at the bars and brothels, buying him drinks, introducing him to prostitutes, and always conversing in that sweet low voice that pulled information out of the intoxicated Mark Handel like honey from a jar.

*   *   *

When Sergeant Sotto sat down with Jorge Manuel, and relayed all that he had learned, and handed him the transcripts of his conversations with Melissa Leaf and Mark

Handel, Jorge Manuel was, to put it mildly, stunned. First, he was stunned by Sergeant Sotto's amazing ability to beguile so much information out of two people, but moreover, he was stunned that an enterprise such as CGI pornography could even exist, much less exist in his antiquated city of La Chorrera. Certainly, Jorge Manuel embraced technology—even his own house had Wi-Fi—but considering the idea that realistic pornographic films could be produced on a computer, well... he would need some time to wrap his head around that.

"This is all very incredible, Sergeant Sotto," Jorge Manuel said, "and I must commend your excellent work. I will certainly remember this when the city council reviews our budget and the requested raises for next year. I must also tell don Fernando of your impressive work."

"Thank you, capitán," whispered Sergeant Sotto.

"But tell me, Sergeant: what is your opinion of the connection between the señor Leaf's film-making business and his death?"

"I could find no connection, capitán. I only included so much detail because once his business partner, señor Handel, started drinking, he would not shut up. He loved to brag so much about how smart he was in protecting this Fig Leaf business that he simply forgot he was speaking with a police officer. Of course, I never wore my uniform when I went to see him."

"Of course not, sergeant. Very smart of you," said Jorge Manuel.

"But there is more, capitán. I interviewed the coroner, the one who performed the autopsy on the late señor Leaf. I did not learn anything more than you already told me, that an undetermined amount of tetrahydrozoline was found in the body. But I did learn that the coroner received not one, but two requests for an official death certificate from two different insurance companies. I thought that was rather strange. So I contacted both insurance companies. Neither one wanted to talk with me until I threatened them, but eventually they both told me why they each needed death certificates. It turns out that there were two life insurance policies taken out on the late señor Leaf—one by his wife Melissa, and one by señor Handel. I don't think either Melissa Leaf or Mark Handel knew that the other one had life insurance on Isaiah Leaf. These were two different insurance companies in two different states in the US, and the policies were taken out at two different times. I don't know if Isaiah Leaf knew about the policies, either. They were the kind of life insurance that doesn't require the consent of the person being insured... the kind that only a spouse or business partner can take out."

"Really?" said Jorge Manuel. "How much were the insurance policies for?"

Sergeant Sotto looked at a small notebook. "Melissa Leaf had insured her husband's life for ten million dollars; and Mark Handel had insured señor Leaf's life for fifteen million dollars."

"Wow!" exclaimed Jorge Manuel. "That's a lot of money."

Sergeant Sotto nodded. "Yes, certainly enough for a motive," he said.

"What about the tetrahydrozoline? Any idea where that came from?" Jorge Manuel asked.

"No, I have had no luck there, but I am still pursuing it. All of the pharmacies in town sell some type of eye drops that contain that chemical. I talked with the pharmacists nearest to where both Melissa Leaf and Mark Handel live. I got copies of both Melissa Leaf's and Mark Handel's passport photos from Immigration and showed them to the pharmacists, but they don't remember them. They both get so many customers; they do not remember anyone in particular. But I have more pharmacies to interview."

Jorge Manuel nodded then said, "I think that connecting this tetrahydrozoline to someone is the only way we can solve this case, Sergeant Sotto. All we really have is a mysterious death and two people who would gain financially from his death. But the insurance is really not enough. Many couples have insurance policies on their spouses, and so do many business partners. Did señor Leaf have any enemies?"

"Ah, an interesting question, capitán. I asked his wife that, and she said no. She said her husband was a sweet man, that he did not have an enemy in the world, that everyone liked him. But when I asked Mark Handel the same question, he told me that señor Leaf had many enemies, that he was so competitive in the pornography business that everyone hated him. It was as if Melissa Leaf and señor Handel were talking about two entirely different people."

"Interesting," mused Jorge Manuel. "Did señor Handel think anyone in particular hated Isaiah Leaf enough to kill him?"

"Oh, he said that many people wanted him dead, but the only name he gave me was a certain Otto Loring."

"And who is this Otto Loring?" ask Jorge Manuel.

"He is a young man from Germany, a competitor in the CGI pornography business," said Sergeant Sotto, "but evidently not a very good one. Señor Handel called him an upstart, and said he made very amateurish CGI movies that no one wanted because they were not realistic. Señor Handel said that this Otto Loring was very jealous of Isaiah Leaf. He told me that Otto Loring started off a few years ago writing very complimentary letters to Isaiah Leaf, praising his work, and asking for a job as an assistant. When Isaiah Leaf turned him down, this Otto Loring became very insistent, trying to get into contact daily with señor Leaf. He wanted to meet with señor Leaf, but señor Leaf kept ignoring him. Señor Handel told me that recently, Otto Loring's emails had become very threatening."

"Did Isaiah Leaf ever meet with him?" Jorge Manuel asked.

"Not that we know of, capitán. We are still checking if Otto Loring has visited Panama recently."

"Yes. Good," Jorge Manuel said. "Let me ask you this, sergeant. What did Melissa Leaf think of this Otto Loring?"

"She told me that she never heard of him."

"Interesting," said Jorge Manuel. "The husband shares these threatening emails with his business partner, but not with his wife."

"Yes, capitán, I thought that was odd, too."

Jorge Manuel furrowed his brow and then said, "It's a shame that the body was cremated so quickly. Don Fernando's friend señor Landes said that if we could have determined the amount of tetrahydrozoline in Isaiah Leaf's body, we would a clearer idea whether this was an accident or intentional."

"Yes, capitán. And to that point, I asked the coroner why the body was cremated so quickly. He told me that it was Melissa Leaf who requested the body be cremated right away."

"Really?" said Jorge Manuel.

"Yes, she claimed she didn't have enough money to pay for a funeral and burial."

CHAPTER THREE

It would not be accurate to describe Ricardo as a porn enthusiast. He did not collect porn, nor did he subscribe to Pornhub, nor anyone's OnlyFans account. Unlike Isaiah Leaf and Mark Handel, Ricardo was not a porn addict. Of course, he appreciated a good money shot as much as the next man, but the fact of the matter was that he didn't think about porn much at all. But it would be accurate to describe Ricardo as a sex enthusiast, and he loved sex with both men and women, and thus, he was familiar with porn. It's hard to be a liberated devotee of pansexuality without being exposed to porn. Gay and bisexual porn movies played constantly in the gay bathhouse in La Chorrera, on endless loops. And thus, when men were lounging about in the large video rooms in the bathhouse, it was common to critique the different porn movies, the plot lines, the cinematography, the best scenes, etc. Additionally, Ricardo traveled to Europe each year, to escape Panama's rainy season; and unlike the US and Latin America, porn was readily accessible and acceptable in Europe, and likewise played constantly on large screens in the gay bars, the cruising rooms, the adult theatres, the sex clubs, the swingers clubs, the bathhouses, and occasionally on late night TV. And so, dear reader, it should not come as a surprise to you to learn that Ricardo was familiar with Fig Leaf Cybernetic films. He didn't know the man behind Fig Leaf Cybernetics; he had only heard the name Isaiah Leaf for the first time at his lucky lottery dinner two weeks earlier; he hadn't made the connection between Isaiah

Leaf—the dead man—and Fig Leaf Cybernetics; but Ricardo was certainly familiar with Fig Leaf Cybernetics films. Had he known that the creator of so many fine porn movies that he admired had moved to La Chorrera nearly a year and a half ago, Ricardo surely would have sought out a way to meet him, to shake his hand, and to tell him what a fan he was of Fig Leaf Cybernetic films. And Ricardo would not have been alone in such admiration.

For it was not just that Fig Leaf porno films were realistic that made them popular; it was the fact that they were *interesting*. The CGI people who inhabited them were *interesting* to look at. The fact is, gentle Reader, that most regular porn films with real actors and real actresses... well, they're boring. There is a certain physical type of person who is willing—and able—to work in the adult film business. If they are guys, they are fit, muscular, square-jawed, short-hair, white, and—I'll say it—*kind of stupid looking*. These are actors who are usually well-endowed but lack any indications of education, culture, personality, or consciousness. If they are women, they pretty much all look the same: young, big tits, and—again—a dumb expression on their faces. And certainly, none, and I mean *none*, of the real men and women who work in porn films can act. The genius of Isaiah Leaf's computer creations is that his people looked intelligent; they looked interesting; each one of them looked different, like a real human being, and not some cookie-cutter porn actor or actress. They looked relatable; they looked emotionally available; and they seemed personally invested in having sex. Imagine the hottest sex you ever had—when both of you really wanted to devour each other: That's the kind of energy that Isaiah Leaf's computer-generated actors appeared to have. People always had the same comment at the end of one of Isaiah Leaf's film: "*That* was hot!"

Of course, the other thing that made Isaiah's films so unique, so easily identifiable, were the camera angles. In filming a real-life porn movie with real people, it is difficult to move the video camera around legs and arms to get the best video angle. Something, or someone, is always in the way. Someone's leg blocks the view, or someone's hair falls and hides their face... but in a CGI film, none of that happens because there is no camera. Isaiah Leaf could program his viewing angle anywhere he wanted, to get the perfect wide-open crotch shot, the perfect money shot, the perfect bukkake shot done in exquisite slow motion. Fig Leaf Cybernetic films were readily identifiable by these beautiful camera angles that would be just impossible to get in real life.

And so it was that Ricardo was familiar with Fig Leaf Cybernetics. And, as fate would have it, that very subject came up when he and his friend Dan Landes were having lunch in Villa Rosario, just a few days after Jorge Manuel had met with Sergeant Sotto.

"Anything new in the world of Panamanian crime?" Ricardo happened to ask Dan as they sat in the restaurant waiting for their food to arrive.

"Well, kind of," Dan replied. "Remember that dead man that Jorge Manuel was telling us about at your lottery dinner?

"Oh yeah," said Ricardo. "You thought he had some odd drug in his blood, tetra-something."

"Tetrahydrozoline," said Dan.

"And what exactly is that, anyway?" Ricardo asked.

"It's a decongestant. It's commonly used in eye drops or nasal sprays. It narrows blood vessels, so eye drop companies use it to take out the redness in eyes. But, like I told Jorge Manuel at dinner, if you ingest this drug, it can fuck with your heart."

"Why would anyone drink eye drops?" Ricardo asked.

"Well, that's the point," Dan replied. "They wouldn't. Someone would have to slip it into their drink, and it wouldn't take much. Anyway, remember at dinner, Jorge Manuel was telling me that the reason he asked for an autopsy was because he had a hunch about the guy's wife, that her grieving didn't seem real to him?"

"No, I don't remember that," said Ricardo. "I only started listening when you said they guy might have been murdered."

"Well," Dan said, "the reason that Jorge Manuel ordered an autopsy was because he had a hunch about the wife. Anyway, it turns out that the wife had taken out a ten million dollar life insurance policy on the guy; and it also turns out that she pressured the coroner to release the body to her fast so she could have it cremated; and she told the coroner that the reason she wanted cremation was that she couldn't afford a funeral and a burial... but the catch is, these people had tons of money. They were loaded."

"Yeah?" said Ricardo, "what did they do?"

"Well, they ran a company called Fig Leaf Cybernetics, and..."

"Wait!" exclaimed Ricardo. "Fig Leaf Cybernetics, the porn film company?"

"You've heard of them?" asked Dan.

"Fuck yes! They're the best!" exclaimed. "They were here in Panama?!"

Dan nodded. "Yes, this Isaiah Leaf fellow, his wife, and his business partner all moved to La Chorrera about a year and a half ago."

"No fucking way!" Ricardo exclaimed. "In La Chorrera? Why didn't you tell me this before? I would have loved to have met them. Fig Leaf Cybernetic films are the best pornos in the world!"

Dan laughed and said, "Well, I only heard of the film company yesterday! I was having lunch with don Fernando, and Jorge Manuel drove in from La Chorrera to join us and update us on his investigation into this guy's death."

"Oh, tell me everything!" gushed Ricardo.

"Well, first tell me what you know about Fig Leaf Cybernetics," said Dan, "because I'd never heard of them until Jorge Manuel told me."

"Well," said Ricardo, "they make CGI porn, you know, computer-generated porn films. But they are so realistic, so believable, you would never know that they were not real people. I first saw one of their films about, I don't know, eight or nine years ago, when I was in Europe. I thought it was the best porno I had ever seen. I had no idea it was all computer-generated. Anyway, Fig Leaf Cybernetic films are very popular in Europe. You can find them everywhere that they show porn. I mean, they must dominate at least thirty percent of the market in Europe, and they have a huge share of the Asian derivative market."

"What do you mean—derivative market?" asked Dan.

"Well," Ricardo explained, "whenever Fig Leaf Cybernetics had a good film, let's say for the American market, they could simply press a few computer buttons, and generate a second film for the French market, where the same people on the screen spoke French, and I don't mean dubbing in a second language—I mean, their mouths would move to actually speak French. Or let's say, they wanted to market the film in Japan. They would press a few more buttons and the actors and actresses would transform into Japanese people. They would look and speak Japanese. These are the derivative porn markets—where you take one completed film and derive dozens of other films out of it. I mean, the plots and motions are all the same, but the actors on screen would look and speak entirely differently. That's why Fig Leaf Cybernetics was so profitable: they could take one film and rebrand it— transform it—into dozens of other high quality porn films for other countries with zilch overhead. It was all pure profit."

"Wow," said Dan. "That's pretty amazing."

"Yeah," said Ricardo, "they were unrivaled. Their only problem that I know of, was that a guy sued them a few years back... He had a funny name, um, Loring, that's it. Otto Loring Productions. Otto Loring was, and I guess still is, a competitor in the CGI porn movie industry. Anyway, this Loring guy sued Fig Leaf Cybernetics, claiming that Fig

Leaf had stolen his proprietary software. It got thrown out of court right away because it was bullshit. Fig Leaf Cybernetics had been making CGI porno before this Loring guy even got out of high school."

"Interesting," said Dan. "Well, Otto Loring's name came up yesterday. Jorge Manuel said that this Loring guy had been sending Isaiah Leaf a bunch of threatening emails recently."

"I think that Loring guy is lawsuit-happy," Ricardo responded. "I've heard he sues everyone. He tried to make it as a porn actor in the US but couldn't get hired because he wasn't... um... well-endowed enough, you know. You gotta be hung like a horse to make it in the porn world. Anyway, anytime someone didn't hire him, he would sue them. He tried to sue them under the Americans with Disabilities Act. It was hilarious. He was a big joke in the porn world, because he was such a dumb fuck. He tried to claim that not being well hung was a disability, and that the porn movie producers had to make a special accommodation for him because of this *quote* disability *unquote*. He got laughed out of court, of course. And he got blacklisted by all porno producers. So, when that career didn't work out, he turned to making CGI porn, but the quality of his stuff is so poor."

"Interesting," said Dan. "Well, he made it onto the suspect list in this case, because, like I said, he had been sending threatening emails to Isaiah Leaf, and then Jorge Manuel checked with Immigration, and it turns out that he entered Panama about a week before Isaiah Leaf died."

"Really?" asked Ricardo. "Is he in La Chorrera?"

"We don't know," said Dan. "He didn't fly into Panama City like most tourists. He came over on a bus from Costa Rica and crossed at the Paso Canoas border crossing."

"He didn't have the money to fly in?" Ricardo asked.

"That might have been it," said Dan, "but it might have been something more devious. When you fly into Panama City, you have to give Immigration your travel plans, like the name of the hotel where you'll be staying, who to contact in case of an emergency, etc. But when you cross overland at Paso Canoas, you don't have to do that. They just record your passport and wave you in. Panama just assumes that any gringos who cross by bus at Paso Canoas are just doing a visa run, where they stay in Paso Canoas overnight and then catch the next bus back to Costa Rica in the morning to get another ninety days on their Costa Rican visa. But Otto Loring didn't exit the next day; in fact, he hasn't exited Panama yet. He's still here, but we don't know where. We've got an alert at all the borders to stop him and interview him if he tries to leave the country. We can't arrest him; we don't have any evidence that he's done anything beyond those threatening emails. We don't even know if he even met with Isaiah Leaf, but we can interview him. Immigration gave us a copy of his passport photo. They have notified all the airports and border crossings where someone could leave the country. If he tries to leave the country, he will be detained long enough for an interview."

"So, you think either Otto Loring or Isaiah's wife might have slipped this Isaiah guy that tetra stuff?" asked Ricardo.

"Well, they both had motive. One of Jorge Manuel's men interviewed the wife's neighbor who said that Isaiah and his wife had lots of loud arguments."

"Hmm... are those your only two suspects?"

"Well," said Dan, "we also have his business partner, a guy named Mark Handel. Turns out he had also taken a large life insurance policy out on Isaiah Leaf. So, he's a distant third on my list of suspects."

"I see," said Ricardo. "So, you and don Fernando are helping Jorge Manuel on this case?"

"Don Fernando is," said Dan. "I'm just listening and giving him advice when I have any."

"And what does don Fernando think about this case?" Ricardo asked.

"He thinks the same as me—that's it's too early to tell. He did ask Jorge Manuel to give him Melissa Leaf's cell phone number."

"That's the wife?" Ricardo asked.

"Yup. Don Fernando's got some whiz-tech computer guy on his staff through some kind of grant from the FBI. This guy can hack into anyone's cell phone."

"Is that legal?" Ricardo asked.

"No," Dan said, "but you know don Fernando. He likes to do everything on an *informal* basis, as he calls it."

"Yeah, I remember," said Ricardo. "But I bet he sucks you into helping on this case. He always does."

"Not this time," said Dan. "I'm too old and retired to get back into the detective game. If Jorge Manuel wants to come to Villa Rosario and bend my ear, I'll listen. If he wants to buy me lunch in La Chorrera, I'll go. But that's the extent of my involvement."

"Unless it gets more interesting," suggested Ricardo.

"Well, yeah... unless it gets more interesting," agreed Dan.

CHAPTER FOUR

The next week delivered three breaks in the case, although none of them really shed any light on how Isaiah Leaf died. The first break came when Sergeant Sotto invited Mark Handel out for a drink, luring him with the promise to take him to a brothel just outside of town, a brothel that Mark hadn't seen yet. This particular brothel, like many such establishments, had a large circular bar in the center, where men could come and have a drink after work. As any experienced brothel madam will tell you, many men need a drink to steady their nerve before picking out a prostitute for the evening. Having a bar inside a brothel gave the men an excuse to go to the address. They could tell themselves that they were just going to have one beer and not to spend their hard-earned money on a hooker. The beer was cheap and cold, and the women would walk around the bar, smiling and making small talk with the men. Eventually, the ever-watchful madam would appear at the side of a potential customer and quietly suggest that such-and-such girl seemed to like the man, and for a small price the man could take her to one of the very convenient rooms that were situated around the bar. The man, having drank several more beers than he intended, was rarely in a position to refuse.

And thus it was that Sergeant Sotto ended up with Mark Handel, sitting at the bar in this particular brothel, drinking beer, and chatting about everything and nothing. As usual, however, there was a method to Sergeant Sotto's ways. At a certain point in the conversation, he pulled out a small plastic bottle of eye drops, tilted his head back, and let a few drops fall into his eyes.

Sergeant Sotto blinked, frowned, and looked at the small plastic bottle in his hand. "This stuff is no good," he said to Mark Handel.

"Oh? What's the matter?" Mark replied.

"Well, smoke really bothers my eyes," Sergeant Sotto explained, "so I bought this bottle to make them feel better. But they don't seem to work."

"What brand are they?" asked Mark as he took another sip of beer.

"They are called *Fácil Ojos*," said Sergeant Sotto, showing Mark the bottle. "That's Spanish for 'Easy Eyes,' but they don't do the trick. They just burn."

"You should try what I use," said Mark, and pulled out a small bottle of Visine from his pants pocket. My eyes get very dry, and this stuff really helps."

Sergeant Sotto took the bottle from Mark's hand and looked at the label. "I've never heard of this brand before," Sergeant Sotto lied. "Where do you get it?"

"You can get it anywhere. I buy mine at the pharmacy next to Chepe's Restaurant. I go through a bottle a week."

"Thanks for the info," said Sergeant Sotto, handing the bottle back to Mark. "I'll have to go there and try it."

Just then, a young Panamanian woman slid up next to Mark, stroked his shoulder and asked, "You men doing okay?" Mark smiled and began to chat with her. Sergeant Sotto didn't mind the interruption, however, because his work for the evening was done.

The next day, a uniformed Sergeant Sotto went to the pharmacy next to Chepe's Restaurant in La Chorrera, showed the pharmacist a photo of Mark Handel, and confirmed that yes, indeed, Mark bought Visine there on a regular basis.

Sergeant Sotto's sense of progress in the case was short-lived, however, because on the following day, he happened to show a photograph of Melissa Leaf to a pharmacist at a different pharmacy, about five blocks from where Melissa lived. That pharmacist recognized the photo of Melissa as someone who had bought eye drops at that pharmacy.

As Sergeant Sotto explained to Jorge Manuel, "I thought I had made a break in the case, capitán, when I discovered that this Mark Handel had bought a lot of eye drops. But this new information cancels out the first break. If both the wife and the business partner bought eye drops, we are no further along in solving this case."

"That is okay, Sergeant," said Jorge Manuel. "Thanks to your good work, we now know that both suspects not only had the motive, but the means of murdering señor Leaf. We just have to keep poking around until we catch another break."

The third break in the case came a day later, when Mark Handel ended up in the hospital. He had had such a good time at that brothel that Sergeant Sotto had taken him to a few days earlier that he decided to return on his own. However, as he was leaving his rented condo, someone jumped out of a nearby doorway and attacked him, beat him severely, and left him lying in the street. An ambulance took him to a nearby hospital. While petty crime is not uncommon in La Chorrera, violent crime is almost unheard of. News of the attack spread quickly. Within an hour, Sergeant Sotto was at the hospital. After listening to Mark Handel's account of what had happened, Sergeant Sotto called Jorge Manuel and asked him to come to the hospital, and to bring a copy of the photo of Otto Loring that they had obtained from Immigration.

Mark Handel had received six stitches to a cut above his eye, and was lying in one of the recovery rooms at the hospital when Sergeant Sotto and Jorge Manuel walked in.

"Mi amigo," said Sergeant Sotto in his soft voice to Mark Handel, "permit me to introduce Jorge Manuel to you. He is the head of the La Chorrera police force. When I told him the dreadful news that you had been attacked, he insisted on personally coming here at once to see you."

Mark and Jorge Manuel shook hands. Mark was not sure why the chief of police would come to the hospital to visit him, but the painkillers that the hospital had given him seemed to make that question not very important.

"Señor Handel," said Jorge Manuel, "on behalf of our town, I extend our deepest apologies for this incident. We do not have crimes like this in La Chorrera. I promise you, we will catch the man who did this."

"Well, thanks, I would appreciate that."

Sergeant Sotto spoke up, "Mi amigo, could you tell my capitán what you told me—about what this man yelled at you while he was beating you? Can you tell him word for word, as best as you remember?"

"Well, he kept calling me a deeb. I had no idea who he was, and it made no sense, but every time he hit me, he called me a—pardon my language—but he called me a fucking deeb. I had no idea what he was talking about. The guy was nuts."

"And you had never seen him before?" asked Jorge Manuel.

"Well, it all happened so fast. But no, I did not know this guy."

Jorge Manuel pulled a photo out of a manila folder and held the photo so that Mark Handel could see it.

"That's him!" exclaimed Mark.

Jorge Manuel and Sergeant Sotto looked at each other. "Do you know who this man is?" Jorge Manuel asked.

"No," said Mark.

"This is Otto Loring," said Jorge Manuel.

"What?!" exclaimed Mark. Then he said to Sergeant Sotto, "That's the guy I told you sent those emails to Isaiah! He tried to sue Isaiah a couple of years ago. Fuck me! I didn't know what he looked like. Isaiah just showed me his emails. That's Otto Loring?! Fuck!"

Jorge Manuel slid the photo back into the manila folder and then put his hand on Mark's shoulder and said, "Señor Handel, I want for you to relax. You need to rest and heal. We will catch this man. The hospital may keep you overnight—I don't know. But I am going to put a man on duty to watch your apartment. And when you go out, I am going to ask Sergeant Sotto to go with you, for your protection. But we will catch this man soon. Do not worry."

"Yeah, okay. Thanks," Mark said. "How did you identify him so fast?"

"Well, señor Handel," Jorge Manuel said, "we are police. That's what we do. We are going to go now. You just rest. I will have one of my men take you home when the hospital releases you."

When Jorge Manuel and Sergeant Sotto had stepped outside of the hospital, Jorge Manuel turned to Sergeant Sotto and asked, "Sergeant, I have to ask: how *did* you know the attacker would turn out to be Otto Loring?"

"It was the word *deeb*, capitán. Señor Handel told me that this attacker kept calling him a deeb. I did not know what that word meant, so I looked it up on the Google, but I got nothing. Then I thought maybe I was spelling it wrong, so I tried different spellings. When I tried d-i-e-b, the Google told me that that was German for thief. I remember you telling me that Otto Loring was originally from Germany and that he claimed señor Leaf had stolen his computer code. So it kind of made sense that he might call señor Leaf's business partner a thief, no?"

"Ah, Sergeant Sotto," said Jorge Manuel, "that is very good poking around, most excellent poking around. Come, let us go to the station and draw up an arrest warrant for this Otto Loring."

CHAPTER FIVE

As mentioned, don Fernando was the police chief of Villa Rosario, and had been the police chief of Villa Rosario for as long as anyone could remember. But more importantly, as also mentioned, he was Jorge Manuel's uncle. Because don Fernando had arranged for the young Jorge Manuel to be appointed police chief of the nearby town of La Chorrera many years ago, it was natural that don Fernando wanted Jorge Manuel to be seen as successful. As such, he often meddled in Jorge Manuel's business, but, to be fair, Jorge Manuel always appreciated don Fernando's help.

As fate would have it, don Fernando had applied for, and received, a grant from the FBI the year before to hire an electronics forensic expert. And he had hired Carlos Wang, a half-Latino, half-Chinese computer guru. And so it was that when Jorge Manuel gave don Fernando Melissa Leaf's cell phone number, don Fernando passed it on to Carlos Wang, and officer Wang undertook what don Fernando would call an *informal* search of Melissa Leaf's call history. Nothing is really illegal in Panama—things are either formal or informal—that's just the way it is. Panamanians and gringos alike have as much privacy as fate allows them, and as far as don Fernando was concerned, if God had not wanted him to learn of Melissa Leaf's call history, God would not have caused the FBI to give him the money to hire the most excellent Carlos Wang.

And so it came to pass that don Fernando called Jorge Manuel to share the good news.

"Koke," said don Fernando, using Jorge Manuel's family nickname, "I have interesting news on your gringo Leaf case."

"Yes, uncle," said Jorge Manuel, "I hope it is good news. I could use some good news. We have circulated the arrest warrant for this Otto Loring, but so far... nothing. We know he is still in the country, but we have no idea where."

"I am sure you will catch him eventually," said don Fernando. "These things take time. But I call today about the wife, the Melissa Leaf. You know how you told me that she told Sergeant Sotto what a happy marriage she and señor Leaf had?"

"Yes, uncle."

"Well, two weeks before señor Leaf died, this happy wife made many calls to a certain phone number in Los Angeles, California, to the law office of a certain señor Lawrence Robertson. And do you know what type of law señor Robertson does? He does divorce law, Koke. And the pattern of her calls is very interesting. Before she called señor Robertson, she called six or seven other divorce lawyers, but only called each of them once. But after she called señor Robertson, she called him back five more times, and each call lasted at least thirty minutes. Then, three days before señor Leaf died, she sent three thousand dollars to señor Robertson via PayPal. Now Koki, tell me, why does someone send that much money to an attorney she has just met?"

"As a retainer, uncle, a retainer for a divorce case," responded Jorge Manuel.

"Very good, Koke. That's exactly what I thought," said don Fernando.

Jorge Manuel was silent for a moment, then asked, "But uncle, if she decided she was going to divorce him, and if she went as far as to send this attorney so much money, why would she turn around and kill her husband a few days later?"

Now it was don Fernando's turn to be silent and think. "That is a very good point, Koke. I do not know the answer to that. But I do think it is time we had an official talk with this Melissa Leaf. I think we have gone as far as we can using Sergeant Sotto's soft approach. Why don't you invite this woman to your police station, and I will come and help you interview her. We can use that 'good cop bad cop' technique I have been reading about. I will threaten to arrest her, and you can be the good cop and stop me."

"I don't know, uncle," said Jorge Manuel. "This woman is very rich, and she is a gringa, and Sergeant Sotto tells me that she is very smart. Plus, we really have no evidence to threaten her with. I don't think using the 'good cop bad cop' technique is going to work. Why don't you bring your friend Dan Landes with you? He is a gringo, and he is good at catching people in lies."

Don Fernando was silent again as he weighed Jorge Manuel's suggestion. Finally, he said, "Ah Koke, yes, that is a good idea. Yes, you are right. It is not like the good old days anymore. Times have changed. Let me talk to Dani and see if I can persuade him to do us this little favor."

And thus it was that Dan Landes, despite his best intentions not to get involved in the Isaiah Leaf case, ended up sitting in the passenger seat of don Fernando's police car the next day as they headed towards La Chorrera.

"I don't know how you always talk me into these things," Dan was saying.

"Ah Dani, it is because I need your help, just this little favor this one time. Koke tells me that this Melissa Leaf is rather arrogant, that she acts like she thinks she is better than us Panamanians. Koke thought it would be best if you took the lead and interviewed her. I have not met this woman, and we really have no evidence to arrest her on, but time is slipping away, and she can leave the country any time she wants, and then we will never have the chance to find out what she knows, and the spirit of her dead husband will have to wander about through all eternity without his murderer being caught."

"You're so full of shit," Dan responded. "I'll do this one interview, but that's it. Now, let's go over this again. She told Jorge Manuel that she had a very strong marriage, but she's been talking to a divorce lawyer in LA..."

"Well, she told Sergeant Sotto she had a strong marriage, and Sergeant Sotto told Koke," interrupted don Fernando.

"Whatever," said Dan. "She claimed she had a strong, loving marriage but she's been consulting a divorce attorney?"

"Right."

"And she paid the divorce attorney three thousand dollars three days before Isaiah Leaf died?"

"Right."

"And the neighbors said they heard the couple arguing a lot?"

"Right."

"And she had her husband's body cremated as soon as the coroner was done with it, and she told the coroner that she wanted it cremated because she didn't have enough money for a funeral and burial, yet she's obviously rich?"

"Right."

"That's not really much to go on, don Fernando," Dan said.

"Well, and don't forget Dani, she had a ten-million-dollar life insurance policy on her husband."

"Nothing illegal about that, don Fernando," said Dan. "Actually, that's pretty common in the United States."

"Really?" exclaimed don Fernando, and then he laughed. "It's a good thing we do not do that here in Panama, or else we would have so many deaths."

When don Fernando and Dan arrived at the La Chorrera police station, Jorge Manuel came out to greet them and took them to an interview room in the back of the station.

"Melissa Leaf will be here shortly," Jorge Manuel explained. "Sergeant Sotto is bringing her, but they have been delayed. Sergeant Sotto called me and said that Melissa Leaf insisted they stop at a Starbucks."

"You have a Starbucks in La Chorrera?" Dan exclaimed. "When did that happen?"

"Quite recently," Jorge Manuel beamed. "Our little town is growing."

"What is a Starbucks?" asked don Fernando.

"It's a US coffee store," explained Dan. "You can buy all kinds of coffee drinks there."

"Is it better than Panamanian coffee?" asked don Fernando.

"Well, they use Panamanian coffee," said Dan. "They import Panamanian coffee to the US, roast it and grind it up there, and then ship it back down here to make coffee."

Don Fernando stared at Dan. "That makes no sense, Dani. We can roast our own coffee and grind it here. Are the coffee drinks they sell cheaper than local coffee?"

"Oh no," laughed Dan. "In fact, it's two or three times as expensive as your local coffee shop."

Don Fernando just shook his head. "Nothing you gringos do makes any sense to me."

Just then Sergeant Sotto appeared at the door with Melissa Leaf, who was wearing sunglasses and holding a cup of Starbucks coffee. The three men who were seated in the interview room all stood up.

Now, as you know, dear Reader, Dan Landes was not what you would describe as a young man. He had been around for many years. He had acquired a certain degree of self-control. He knew how to handle social situations. And, as an ex-detective, he knew how to handle all different types of suspects in an interview, including beautiful women. And he fully expected Melissa Leaf to be good looking. He knew that she had been a porn starlet, and he knew that rich men like Isaiah Leaf always marry beautiful women. But he was not prepared for how stunningly beautiful Melissa Leaf was when she entered that interview room. There was something about her that seemed to suck the air right out of him. There was something about her auburn hair, her jaw line, the color of her lips, her neck, her clothes, even the perfect subliminal hint of her perfume. Everything about her was just perfect and seemed to click some internal yearning in him. For a brief microsecond, he felt bowled over. Luckily, she was busy setting her coffee cup down on the table and did not seem to notice his reaction to her. He tried to compose himself right away, because he had promised don Fernando and Jorge Manuel that he would conduct the interview.

"Mrs. Leaf," Dan said, "thank you so much for coming in. We apologize for inconveniencing you, especially so soon after the unfortunate passing of your husband. We all extend our deepest condolences. Please, let me introduce you to everyone: This is Jorge Manuel, the chief of police of this town; and this is José Fernando, the chief of police of Villa Rosario, the next town over; and I am Dan Landes. I'm just an expat who happens to have lived here for a long time, and so occasionally the police use me rather than hire a translator. Between you and me, they just use me because it saves them money. Please, have a seat."

Melissa Leaf took a seat, leaving her sunglasses on. Sergeant Sotto left the room, closing the door behind him. The three remaining men sat down. Dan Landes looked up to the ceiling to try and focus on his years of interview experience, and then he continued.

"Mrs. Leaf, the reason we asked you to come in and talk with us is that we have a concern about the death of your husband. I'm going to tell you everything we know. And because these gentlemen sitting here with me today are policemen, they know a lot. Some of what they know will be things you already know, but you will be surprised that we know it; some of what they know may come as a shock to you; some of what they know may worry you; but I'm going to be completely honest with you because we are missing some pieces.

"So, here's what we know: We know that your husband and his partner Mark Handel ran Fig Leaf Cybernetics. We are intimately aware of the nature of the business that Fig Leaf Cybernetics is involved in, and let me reassure you that that business—the business of CGI pornography—does not concern us here. We know that Isaiah wrote computer code for hundreds of extremely popular, X-rated, straight, gay, trans, you-name-it pornography, and to be direct—*we don't care*. The legal questions posed by computer-generated pornography are light years ahead of anything the Panamanian legal system has ever dealt with, and more importantly, no pornography was ever filmed inside Panama's borders. The only thing that was ever created here was computer code, and Panama has no laws against that. We know that Isaiah had a whole bank of computer servers in Nevada. We know his distribution system was headquartered in the Caymen Islands. We know that Fig Leaf Cybernetics was not even technically owned by your late husband. No amount of Panamanian lawyers or accountants could ever navigate through the layers of offshore shell companies that makes up Fig Leaf Cybernetics. Let me stress again that we don't care about any of that."

Melissa Leaf tilted her head, and then took off her sunglasses. Dan was surprised by two things: first, how green her eyes were—deep shimmering green— and secondly, how those deep green irises were floating in a sea of red. Her eyes were bloodshot. She had been crying. Evidently, whatever eyedrops she might have been using weren't enough to remove the red.

"Then why am I here?" she asked. She squinted at the glare of the overhead florescent lights and slipped her sunglasses back on.

"Your husband died of a heart attack," Dan answered, "but we have reason to believe the heart attack was induced by a drug that somehow found its way into his food or his drink. The coroner found traces of tetrahydrozoline in Isaiah's blood."

Dan paused to watch Melissa Leaf's reaction. Her jaw dropped ever so slightly; her lips parted ever so slightly as she took in a tiny gasp of air; her torso retracted ever so slightly—as if she was flinching from someone's attempted punch; and her head jutted forward ever so slightly. These were ever-so-small involuntary movements—"tells" they call them in poker—and they were authentic reactions—Dan could tell that much—but he couldn't tell whether she was reacting because of the suggestion that her husband might have murdered, or whether she was reacting because the police had discovered the tetrahydrozoline.

"What—what are you saying?" she blurted.

"I am simply saying that there was tetrahydrozoline in your husband's blood, enough of this drug to indicate that he had consumed it, and it's not a drug that one knowingly consumes because... it's poisonous, and even a small amount can induce a heart attack. In the world of infinite possibilities, it is possible that, somehow, he accidentally consumed a small, but lethal, amount of tetrahydrozoline. In the world of accidents, anything is possible. Tetrahydrozoline is a drug that is commonly found in eye drops. Did your husband have problems with his eyes, Mrs. Leaf?"

"Well... yes. He worked on his laptop all day long, every day. His eyes would get tired. He kept a bottle of eyedrops on his desk. In fact, we both used eye drops..."

Melissa stopped midsentence, then said, "You're not saying he was murdered, are you?"

"We don't know, Mrs. Leaf. We are trying to get a complete picture," Dan said. "I told you that I will tell you everything we know. We are hoping you can fill in some of the missing pieces for us."

Dan could tell Melissa was looking downward. Her head moved left then right in micromovements. Dan imagined those green eyes behind the sunglasses sweeping back and forth, a telltale sign that someone is thinking.

"As I said, tetrahydrozoline is commonly found in eye drops, and eye drops can be purchased at any pharmacy. We know that you use eyedrops, and that you buy them from the Mora Pharmacy located about five blocks from your condo. We know that Mark Handel also buys eye drops from a pharmacy near his residence. Anyone can buy eye drops. And we also know that your husband had many enemies. You told Sergeant Sotto that Isaiah did not have any enemies, but we know that in fact, he had many. His business partner, Mr. Handel, described for us the fiercely competitive business that Fig Leaf Cybernetics was engaged in. We know of some threatening emails that your husband received recently from one such competitor, one Otto Loring. We know that Otto Loring entered Panama recently, and that, in fact, he attacked and beat Mark Handel last night, beat him to the point that he had to go to the hospital and get stitches to his head. He is alright now; he is resting at home, and we are guarding his residence. We have a warrant out for Otto Loring's arrest."

Melissa Leaf took off her sunglasses and stared at Dan, her mouth open. "Wha—what?! This happened to Mark last night? What—how badly was he hurt?"

"He'll be alright," Dan replied. "Nothing broken, but he's got six stitches over his left eye, but he'll recover."

"Oh my God!" said Melissa. Dan noticed that the color had drained from her face. Dan turned to Jorge Manuel and asked, in Spanish, if Jorge could have some water brought into the interview room. Jorge stood up, left the room, and returned with a glass of water for Melissa.

"Thank you," she said and took a sip.

"So, tell me, how long were you and your husband married?" Dan asked.

"It would have been ten years next month," Melissa said softly.

"Was your husband depressed lately? Was he drinking heavily, or did he show any indications of wanting to take his own life?"

"No, not at all. Things were going well. His business was flourishing. And Isaiah never drank. In fact, people used to comment about Isaiah's and Mark's friendship. Isaiah would never take a drink or use drugs, and Mark was a party animal—he was always drinking. But they were best friends."

"And how were things between you and Isaiah lately?"

"They were fine," said Melissa curtly.

Dan leaned forward, "Mrs. Leaf, we know that you've had several lengthy conversations with Lawrence Robertson, a well-known divorce attorney in Los Angeles. We know that you sent him a three-thousand-dollar retainer the week before your husband died. So, I will ask you again, how was the marriage lately?"

Tears began to well up in Melissa Leaf's eyes. Don Fernando slid a box of tissues over to her. She dabbed at her eyes and said, "They were not good. I mean, the marriage was good, I loved Isaiah, but I decided I had to leave—for my own safety."

Melissa began to cry softly. Dan just waited. A full minute passed. Finally, Melissa spoke. "Isaiah had decided to take the business to a new level. He had been spending more and more time on the dark web. He had been working on this project for the last few months. He had created several different accounts using Freenet and Tor browsers—he was convinced he could be totally undetected. He had run several business models—trial balloons he called them—and he had decided he could take Fig Leaf Cybernetics *completely deep*, he called it."

Don Fernando and Jorge Manuel looked at Dan. He could tell they had no idea what the dark net was or what Freenet and Tor were. But Dan knew.

"To what end?" Dan asked.

Melissa looked completely distraught. Dan had seen this look many times in police interviews. There was something that she wanted to share, but she was scared to say it out loud.

Dan took a chance and said, "There's no reason not to tell us now, Mrs. Leaf. Your husband is gone. Whatever plans he had for the dark web aren't going to happen."

Melissa held back a sob, wiped away her tears, took a breath, and said: "Fig Leaf Cybernetics had always stayed in the adult film business. Isaiah's films were explicit, they were graphic, they were definitely triple-X rated, but they were always legal, and they were artistic—that's what first drew me to Isaiah. He was an artist. But the films were always adult... adult!... adult!... all of his creations looked adult. He never went towards the 'barely legal' market. Mark always was able to keep Isaiah fenced in, focused on the core business, the main cash flow of just making adult films using simulated adult actors. Isaiah sold thousands of DVDs in Europe and Asia, and he had a good streaming business to US adult venues. Isaiah's films made tons of money, not only because he was the best, but because he was the best *and* the cheapest. He had no fucking overhead! He and Mark were grossing over four million dollars a year. We had more money than we could spend..."

Melissa wiped away more tears.

"But Isaiah began to change. It wasn't enough money. I kept telling him that we were so fortunate, that we should be so happy, that we could retire now. But this last year, his profits began to dip. There is so much competition from free porn. He wanted to do ad placements in his films but that didn't work. He tried to set up an Only Fans account using CGI models, but he couldn't make the CGI react fast enough to the live cam questions from viewers. So then, he started investigating the dark web. I told him no, that it wasn't safe, that it wasn't right, but he kept at it."

Melissa was sobbing now. Dan was thinking hard. What was it about the dark web that scared Melissa so? What would Isaiah be doing there that he wasn't already doing? Then it dawned on him.

"He wanted to create simulated child porn?" Dan blurted out.

Melissa nodded and started sobbing hard.

Dan leaned back in his chair and took in a deep breath. If Isaiah Leaf had gotten into the child porn business on the dark web, there was no telling how much money he could have made. All those child porn addicts all over the world would have paid billions to have Isaiah Leaf's quality in child pornography films. My God, he thought, it would be like Isaiah owning the entire California gold rush in the wild west. He could have named his own price; he would have had zero competition. He could have taken his already-existing films and, with some computer code, simply changed one or two of the CGI characters into children, and presto, instant child pornography. It was staggering.

Dan sat there silently, thinking about this. Melissa was sobbing quietly. Don Fernando and Jorge Manuel looked confused, but they took their cues from Dan's behavior and just sat silently.

Eventually, Melissa's sobs ended, and she said, "Mark and I both tried to talk him out of it. We both said that we had enough money. But Isaiah wasn't satisfied. I don't think all the money in the world would have been enough for him. And maybe it wasn't the money, I don't know..."

"Was he into child pornography, himself?" Dan asked softly.

"Not that I knew of. I never saw him with any, but lately I had begun to wonder if I knew him at all. He wasn't the man I married. We had lots of fights about it. I keep telling him he would get caught, that they would change the laws just to get him, that he couldn't do child porn and get away with it, but he thought he could. I decided I had to get out of the marriage, so I called around for a divorce attorney. I knew I had to act fast because Isaiah said he was going to launch his first dark web film in sixty days."

"Did you tell him that you were going to divorce him?" Dan asked.

Melissa shook her head no.

Mark thought for a moment, then asked, "Did Mark Handel know you were going to divorce Isaiah?"

Melissa shrugged. "I don't know. I told him I was considering it, but I didn't tell him I had decided to do it."

"Was Mark helping him get into the dark web?" Dan asked.

"Oh no... well no, not at first," Melissa said. "Mark was totally against it. Mark may be alcoholic, but he's not stupid. He's a good lawyer. He kept telling Isaiah that it wasn't worth the risk, but Isaiah could not be dissuaded. So, I think Mark may have decided to help him create legal protections, I don't know... I know they talked about ways to protect Isaiah."

Dan nodded. Melissa's answers sounded truthful, and he didn't want to push her any further, but he had a few more questions.

"Did Mark Handel know how to code?" Dan asked. "I mean, was he in any way involved with the creation of any of Isaiah's films?"

Melissa shook her head no. "No," she said, "he had no skill in that area. I mean, he loved porn; he loved watching it. Isaiah would show all of his first drafts of films to Mark, and Mark would critique them and make suggestions. Mark called it 'proofreading'—that's how he would bill Isaiah for critiquing new films, under proofreading..."

"Really?" said Dan. "Mark would bill him for watching porn?"

"Yes," Melissa replied. "I mean, Mark was providing a service, so of course he billed Isaiah. Mark would watch and rewatch every scene and take extensive notes. Mark even suggested dialogue and camera angles. Isaiah would use those notes to improve the scenes. Even though Mark couldn't code his way out of a paper bag didn't mean he wasn't essential to Isaiah's films. Isaiah depended on Mark's critiques, so of course, Mark billed Isaiah for his time.

"So, their relationship was just attorney and client?

"Yup, everything about Mark was on the up and up. He billed for his time. He made sure Isaiah paid the exact taxes he owed. He walked the straight and narrow. He always used to tell Isaiah that to live outside the law, you have to be honest. He was always able to keep Isaiah reined in, that is, until Isaiah got involved in the dark web."

"And your husband never mentioned this Otto Loring?" Dan asked.

"No. I've never heard that name."

"Do you know of any enemies your husband had?" Dan asked.

"No," Melissa said, "but Isaiah never talked business with me."

Dan thought carefully about how to phrase his next question. "Who would have had access to his food or drink?" he asked.

"Neither of us liked to cook, so we ate all of our meals at restaurants, or had it delivered," she answered. "Isaiah often worked late into the evening, and sometimes he would go out for a bite to eat after I had gone to bed."

Dan nodded and said, "Mrs. Leaf, we thank you very much for your time. I am so sorry to put you through this. My understanding from Jorge Manuel is that Sergeant Sotto is going to take you back to your condo. If you don't mind, we would like to post a police car outside your condo. Until we can locate this Otto Loring and arrest him, we don't want to take any chances. I don't think there is any reason to alter your daily routine, but we want to be careful."

Melissa Leaf looked concerned but only said, "I understand."

She stood up and adjusted her sunglasses. The three men stood up, and Jorge Manuel escorted her out of the room. Dan and don Fernando sat back down, each man thinking his own thoughts. When Jorge Manuel came back into the room, don Fernando spoke up.

"I am confused, Dani. This dark web is a website?"

"No, don Fernando, it's more like a space on the internet where everything is encrypted... where encrypted websites can gather. How to explain it?... You know the San Miguelito area in Panama City, where the drug dealers and prostitutes hang out? Where they sell drugs openly on the street and where you can buy stolen cell phones and stolen TVs? The police are too scared to go into that neighborhood, right? And you and I can't wander down those streets—we'd be shot. We'd have to go in some kind of disguise. Well, the dark web is like that. You can only go there if you create an encrypted account for yourself, and you have to use certain platforms to get in. Everything you see there is encrypted. But you can buy drugs there, or porn, or stolen credit cards. It's a wide-open criminal market, all available on your computer. And the police can't stop it because they don't know who anybody is."

Don Fernando looked very concerned. "And there is child pornography for sale there?" he asked.

Dan nodded and said, "Tons of it, don Fernando. In fact, that's where all of it is concentrated."

Jorge Manuel spoke up: "And this Isaiah Leaf was going to make child pornography to sell on this dark web?"

Dan nodded. "Sounds like that was *exactly* what he was going to do."

"But... but... if he got caught, wouldn't he go to jail for a long time?" Jorge Manuel asked.

"Well, that's an interesting question," Dan said. "First, he would have to be caught. When was the last time you heard of some criminal being caught on the dark web? The last time I remember a porn kingpin being busted for selling child porn on the dark web was maybe in 2015. The dark web is all encrypted; all payments are handled in bitcoin; and those bitcoins are washed in internet tumblers so that they are not traceable; the child porn itself is encrypted; the people buying it are using encrypted accounts... I mean, the FBI would have to set up a sting operation, create their own encrypted account, and make a purchase on the dark web, but even then, how would they prove who they bought the porn from? How much resources does the FBI have to devote to that kind of project? Ten people? Twenty people? Did you know that there are three million visitors *a day* to the dark web? Millions of encrypted accounts wandering around looking for sex or drugs *every single day*. And then there's the bigger question of whether CGI child porn is even illegal. There are no real children involved. It's basically a cartoon, a very realistic cartoon."

"But Dani," said don Fernando, "it's children. It looks like children. Isn't that illegal?"

Dan shrugged. "Is it?" he asked. "It's just numbers in a computer code. By definition, child pornography has to be pornography involving children. How can it be child pornography if no children are involved?"

Don Fernando shook his head. "It *can't* be right, Dani. It feels so wrong."

"I agree," Dan said, "I'll do some research, don Fernando. It's been too many years since I was a cop. Maybe the laws have changed. Maybe it is illegal. I'll let you know what I find."

"Maybe that's why Isaiah Leaf was killed," Jorge Manuel suggested. "Maybe someone wanted to stop him."

"Maybe," Dan said.

"You know something that bothers me, Dani?" don Fernando said. "This Melissa Leaf, she seemed more upset that Otto Loring had attacked her husband's lawyer than she was when you suggested her own husband had been murdered."

"I noticed that too, don Fernando. I don't know what to make of that. She was amazingly candid with us. She didn't have to tell us anything about the child porn stuff, yet she did. She's a strange woman."

The three men sat silently together, each one lost in his own thoughts.

CHAPTER SIX

When Dan told don Fernando that he would research whether CGI child pornography was illegal, what he meant was that he would call one of his old friends back in the States who would know. Dan had a deep appreciation of his limitations: he was an ex-cop, not a lawyer, and he wouldn't know how to research the current legal status of laws as complicated as those governing pornography. But Dan had a good lawyer friend back in L.A. So the next day, he called Stanley Schneider.

Dan's friendship with Stanley went back to Dan's days as a detective with the L.A. police department. It was a long history that doesn't concern us here. Suffice it to say that they were good friends—it was the kind of friendship where Dan could call Stanley out of the blue for a legal opinion.

"Is CGI child pornography illegal?" said Stanley. "Well, that's a very complicated question."

"Can you simplify it for me? Like maybe a one-sentence answer?" Dan asked.

"One sentence?" Stanley chuckled. "Well, clearly *real* child pornography with real children is illegal, and Congress has tried to pass laws that make *any* depiction of sexual conduct involving children—even drawings—illegal. But those laws have not been tested by the Supreme Court. Personally, I think that if they ever are tested, they will be struck down."

"I see, said the blind man," Dan quipped.

Stanley laughed. "Let me give you the longer answer," he said. "In the legal world, there is a difference between pornography and obscenity. They're totally different. In the US, pornography has always had some First Amendment protection because it's a form of personal expression, a form of free speech. But then, there was a Supreme Court case back in the seventies that said that if a book or film was deemed *obscene*, then it *wasn't* protected by the First Amendment. And so, the question became: what is obscene? and then you got a bunch of court cases that talked about community standards and lack of literary or artistic value, yada yada. So, under *that* definition, *any* type of pornography, child or otherwise, *could be* deemed illegal if it was obscene. Follow me? Pornography wasn't illegal *unless* it was obscene. That was the definition back in the seventies. CGI didn't exist back then, so CGI porn wasn't an issue. And there were a few court cases that exempted cartoons, art, and literature... well, they didn't *exempt* them. They said that they fell under the usual tests of community standards and literary merit. Remember the controversy over the book and the film *Lolita*? Clearly, it's a story about sex with a child. But it wasn't considered obscene because it had literary value, and therefore, not illegal. But then there was this boom in child porn videos in the eighties, and a huge public outcry over them. So, in the early nineties, Congress passed a bunch of laws to make child porn *per se* illegal—I'm talking real child porn, not CGI child porn, because CGI still hadn't been invented yet—but prosecutors ran into obstacles with what I call the 'identifiable victim' problem. If they couldn't prove the person in the video was actually underage, then they couldn't prosecute the filmmaker. So, every time the FBI wanted to make a case, they had to find the person who was in the film and prove that this person was underage when the film was made. It was a mess. So, in the early two-thousands, Congress passed a federal law that tried to twist and cram the term 'child pornography' *under* the definition of obscenity. That way, the prosecutors could argue that it didn't matter if the person in the film was underage or even a real person, as long as the image in the film *looked like* an underage person engaged in sexual conduct, *then* that image was deemed obscene, and therefore illegal. You see what I'm saying? It's real circular reasoning, because, in essence, it says that something is not illegal *because* it's child pornography; it's illegal because it's obscene. And why is it obscene? Because it looks like child pornography. Follow me? So, by defining the *appearance* of a child involved in a sexual act as obscene, Congress was trying to take away the ability of a judge or jury to decide whether a work had literary value. And that law had one sentence that specifically said that drawings or cartoons or paintings that looked like minors having sex were obscene.

"But... that law, and specifically that one sentence in that law, has not been fully tested before the Supreme Court. I mean, there's been a number of convictions under that law, but those cases were all messy, ones where the defendant had a mixture of real child porn and porn cartoons. The legality of that one sentence, that says that a drawing or cartoon that *appears to* depict a minor having sex is obscene *per se*, has not been tested.

"And it may be years before that one sentence is tested. You know how it is: you have to have the perfectcase to get up to the Supreme Court to really test whether a law is constitutional or not. In my view, the law is overbroad. It basically says if someone looks like a child, then they are a child. You get the right case in front of the Supreme Court, and I don't think that law would survive."

"I see," said Dan. "But, if someone produced a cartoon that looked like children having sex, they could be prosecuted?"

"Yes," said Stanley. "They *could be* prosecuted, but, depending on the facts of the case, they might create new law. For example, I've always thought that the perfect case—from a defendant's point of view—would be an animated video of something from the Bible, say, Lot's daughters seducing their father. The Bible just says that Lot's daughters wanted descendants, so they got their father drunk and had sex with him, and both got pregnant. The Bible doesn't say their age; it just says there was an older daughter and a younger daughter. But if you had a nicely animated cartoon that stuck strictly to the biblical verse, *and* showed what appeared to be an underage younger daughter having explicit sex with her father... well, I'd like to see a prosecutor argue to a jury that the Bible had no literary value."

"You've got a twisted sense of humor, Stanley," Dan laughed.

"Ah, I'm just a lawyer," Stanley replied.

Dan paused for a moment, trying to think if he had any other questions for Stanley, but then Stanley spoke up again.

"But Dan, I don't want to leave you with a false impression. Lawyers like to talk about the state of the law in rarified tones, because things seem clearer in the abstract, but the fact is, when you get down to the trial level, in the actual courtroom, things are always messy. Those First Amendment protections exist in legal arguments at the appellate court level. But you get some schmuck with a CGI child porn video in front of a jury, and they won't care about his First Amendment rights. If the jury thinks that guy is making child porn, he's going to get convicted. And he may spend years in jail before his case makes it to the Supreme Court."

"And I suppose," Dan said, "that the more realistic the CGI porn is, the easier it would be for a jury to convict him."

"I would agree with that."

"Hmm, and what about other countries, Stanley?"

"Totally different, Dan. Other countries don't have our First Amendment protections, so a person producing child porn would have very little defense. Some countries have no laws at all on pornography, but of the ones that do, most of them just make the representation—just the appearance—of child pornography illegal, whether it's a real child or not. So, if a person was producing CGI child porn, and it was on the internet for sale, any country in the world that had internet could theoretically prosecute that person. And the fact that it was CGI wouldn't make any difference."

"Okay, Stanley. Thanks man. You were right, it is complicated. But I think I understand it better now."

"Any time, Dan."

After Dan hung up from his call, he just sat at his desk and tried to digest all that Stanley had told him. He thought Melissa Leaf had good reason to want to divorce Isaiah over his decision to put CGI child porn on the dark web. It looked like Isaiah would have less legal protection than he thought he had. And if Isaiah did get arrested, Melissa and Mark would be legally liable, too. Dan wondered why people were never satisfied with what they had. Isaiah had already found success and wealth with Fig Leaf Cybernetics. Why would he want to get involved with something as immoral and risky as the dark web? He had more money than he knew what to do with. He had a beautiful wife. He could have just retired. Dan thought about Melissa some more— those green eyes. She stirred something inside him. He wondered if he would see her again. He shook his head when he realized he was attracted to her. There he was, proving his own point about people never being satisfied with what they have. Melissa was very attractive, but Dan knew better. He knew of too many good detectives back in L.A. who made the mistake of getting involved with witnesses or suspects in a criminal investigation. It *always* ended badly. Those men had lost their jobs. More than a few had lost their wives and families, too. All for a taste of forbidden fruit. Dan shook his head again. Men never change, he thought to himself. The image of Odysseus came to his mind. He remembered the myth of the female sirens of the sea whose song was so haunting it would lure sailors to their death. Odysseus knew that, yet he still wanted to hear their song, and so he ordered his crew to lash him to the mast and to plug their ears with beeswax as they sailed past the sirens. Their song almost drove Odysseus mad. But he still wanted to hear it.

Most of us never get to experience what Odysseus did, Dan thought. Most of us are lashed to different masts, landlocked by fate to careers and lives that never feel the ocean waves propel us to the sirens' temptation. Maybe it's only the rich and powerful that can afford to taste forbidden fruit and get away with it. You only hear of the ones that get caught, like Jeffrey Epstein. You never hear of the millions of rich men who simply buy all the siren songs they want. For some reason, Dan thought of Tiberius Caesar, the emperor of Rome in 26 AD, who kept children for sex at his palace on the Island of Capri. Tiberius Caesar died an old man, in his bed. So much for justice.

Dan wondered what, if anything, would happen next. Probably nothing. Melissa and Mark would probably return to the States, collect on the life insurance policies they had taken out on Isaiah, and retire as multimillionaires. Life in Panama would go on as normal. Dan wondered what would happen to Fig Leaf Cybernetics. Surely it would continue in its layered corporate form, collecting money. After all, all Isaiah's films were still selling. Who would be in charge now? Where would those funds go? Who were Isaiah's beneficiaries? Probably Melissa. Maybe Mark.

Dan made a mental note to ask Jorge Manuel to ask Sergeant Sotto if he could sweet talk that information out of Mark Handel before Mark left Panama. Dan wasn't sure why he was curious about that. This investigation wasn't going anywhere.

61

CHAPTER SEVEN

But two things happened the next day that changed Dan's view of the case. First, the FBI showed up in La Chorrera. Two agents came, unannounced, to visit Jorge Manuel at the La Chorrera police station, with questions about the death of Isaiah Leaf. But Jorge Manuel was shrewder than his young years would indicate. Plus, he had heard stories about the FBI from his uncle don Fernando. Whenever don Fernando spoke about the FBI, he would make this little joke and call it the Federal Burro of Investigation—burro as in donkey. So, instinctively, Jorge Manuel claimed that he wasn't authorized to speak about this case. He told the FBI that don Fernando was actually in charge of the case and gave them directions to drive to Villa Rosario. As soon as the agents left, Jorge Manuel called his uncle and warned him that the FBI were on their way. Don Fernando, in turn, called Dan Landes and asked Dan to come by his office. And thus it was that an hour later, Dan and don Fernando were waiting in the Villa Rosario police station when the two agents showed up.

The weather in Villa Rosario is always hot. Only the level of humidity changes, and it alternates between humid and very humid. On this particular day, as fate would have it, it was very humid. So, not only were the two FBI agents frustrated by having to drive to Villa Rosario, but they were sweating profusely in their suits. Nonetheless, they kept their jackets on, and introduced themselves to don Fernando and Dan when they were shown into don Fernando's office.

"I'm agent Ian Williams and this is agent Brian Dickerson," the taller of the two agents said, as both agents held out their FBI badges.

"Welcome, welcome," don Fernando said effusively. "I am José Fernando, the chief of police of this little town. And this is my friend and colleague, Dan Landes, a gringo like yourselves, who helps me translate when we have visitors from the United States. What an honor it is to have representatives from your wonderful organization come to visit us. I have long admired your FBI. Please come in and have a seat. You must be very tired from your drive in. I will have some lemonade brought in."

Dan smiled and shook the agents' hands but thought to himself that maybe don Fernando was overacting. The fact was, don Fernando's English was quite adequate. But the agents seemed to buy the explanation and took their seats at a small conference table in don Fernando's office. Don Fernando picked up his phone and barked out an order in Spanish for a pitcher of lemonade and four glasses with ice. A police officer carrying a tray with the lemonade appeared immediately as don Fernando and Dan were sitting down at the table.

"Ah, lemonade," don Fernando said, "just the thing on such a hot day. I must apologize for our weather. It gets rather hot in the afternoon."

Don Fernando poured the lemonade and passed around the glasses. The agents looked grateful to be drinking something cold.

"So, gentlemen," don Fernando continued, "to what do we owe the great honor of your visit?"

The taller agent spoke again. Clearly, he was the one in charge. "Well, sir, we are given to understand that you are in charge of the investigation into the death of one Isaiah Leaf."

Don Fernando nodded. "Yes, yes, well… it's Agent Williams, correct? Yes, well Agent Williams, I guess you could say that, yes, although to be honest, *investigation* is not exactly the right word. Whenever anyone dies in our country, the police must make an inquiry. We are, how do you say? a very bureaucratic country. There are forms that must be filled out. But yes, I am in charge of the inquiry."

"And what can you tell us about this man's death?"

"About his death?" don Fernando asked. "Well, he died. He was working at his desk at home, and he just fell over. An ambulance arrived, and the two attendants tried to revive the man. They did, what is it, CBR? on the man, and they rushed him to the hospital. But unfortunately, he was pronounced dead."

"And who identified the body?" Agent Williams asked.

"Identified the body? He died at home. His wife told us she was in the other room and heard him fall to the floor. She called the ambulance immediately. She rode in the ambulance with him to the hospital."

"Was there an autopsy?" Agent Williams asked.

"An autopsy? No, no," said don Fernando. Dan bit the inside of his cheek but held his face calm. He wasn't sure why don Fernando was lying.

"No," don Fernando continued. "The doctors said he had had a heart attack. There was no indication of any foul play, so there was no autopsy."

"Is there a death certificate?" Agent Williams asked.

"Yes, of course." Don Fernando got up, went over to his desk, looked through some manila folders and pulled out a piece of paper.

"Here it is," he said and handed it to Agent Williams. Both agents looked at the document.

"And who signed this death certificate?" Agent Williams asked.

"Let me see," said don Fernando and leaned forward. Agent Williams handed him the document. "Oh yes, Doctor Javier Hugo, a very good doctor, one of the best that we are fortunate to have in the city of La Chorrera."

"I see," said Agent Williams. "And where was the body buried?"

"Buried? No, no, he was a gringo, so his body was cremated," don Fernando said.

The agents looked confused. Don Fernando turned to Dan and said, "Dani, can you explain to these gentlemen why gringos are not buried?"

Dan nodded and said, "You see, there is no embalming here. These towns are too poor to have that service. If a local Panamanian dies, and if the family has prepaid for a crypt or burial plot, then the deceased is simply buried within twenty-four hours of death. Otherwise, the body would start to decompose. The heat and the humidity are just too much. But if a foreigner dies, or if anyone dies without a prepaid crypt, then the body is immediately cremated. That is the practice down here."

The two agents nodded. Agent Dickerson spoke up. "Can we get an official copy of this death certificate?"

"You can have that one," said don Fernando. "It is an extra."

"Is it certified?" Agent Dickerson asked, examining the document.

"Of course. As I told you, we are a very bureaucratic country. Everything is certified."

The two agents seemed to be satisfied with that. They looked as if they were ready to leave. But Dan just had to ask. "You know, you two came a long way just to get a death certificate. You could have called, and Police Chief Fernando would have been happy to send you one.

"Well actually," Agent Williams said, "we tried calling several days in a row, but we kept getting transferred from one person to the next. No one seemed to know anything about this case."

Dan nodded and said, "Ah yes, that's common."

Don Fernando shrugged. "I am sorry, we are a bureaucratic country."

"But still," Dan continued, "why is the FBI interested in this one tourist?

"Well, we're always concerned when an American citizen dies overseas," Agent Williams said.

Dan spoke before he could think. "Well, that's bullshit. The FBI doesn't come traipsing down here just because some middle-aged tourist dies. Police chief Fernando has been gracious with you. The least you could do, as a fellow law-enforcement officer, is to clue him in."

Officer Williams seemed taken aback by Dan's brusque tone, but he nodded, and said, "That's fair. Unfortunately, all I can tell you is that Isaiah Leaf was a person of interest in an investigation."

"An investigation into what?" Dan asked.

"Unfortunately, I can't discuss the details of an ongoing investigation."

"Really?" Dan replied. "The man's dead. That rather closes your investigation, doesn't it?"

Agent Williams nodded. "Well, you have a point there," he said. "But until I get clearance from above, I still can't discuss it."

Don Fernando smiled broadly and spread his hands wide. "Ah, gentlemen," he said. "You work for a bureaucratic organization, too. Yes, we all understand each other. There's no escaping bureaucratic procedures, is there?"

Agent Williams nodded and said, "That's true. But our work here is done. And this document effectively closes our case. We appreciate your hospitality, Chief Fernando. We have a long drive back to Panama City, so we'd better get going."

After the two FBI agents left, don Fernando had some coffee brought into his office and he and Dan sat and talked.

"An interesting visit, eh?" don Fernando said. "Tell me, Dani, why do you think they came all the way to Panama for this one man?"

"They wanted to make sure he was dead," Dan replied. "That's the only possible reason. But that means Isaiah Leaf was very important to whatever they were investigating. I wish they had told us more. By the way, why didn't you tell them about the autopsy?"

"Oh, the autopsy just raises more questions than it answers, Dani. They would have stuck around, bothering us. They might have wanted to interview Javier Hugo, and Javier is an idiot. He would have made us look bad. It's better this way. If something comes up that we need them for, I will call them back and say that I misunderstood the question or that Koke never told me about the autopsy. It's better to keep the FBI on a need-to-know basis."

"Really? I thought you had a relationship with them. Don't you receive several grants from the FBI, don Fernando? Like your new computer tech guy? Didn't the FBI give you money to hire him? And don't they pay for some online courses you've been taking?"

"Yes, Dani, that is exactly the point. The FBI gives me a lot of grant money, but that is because in my applications I make our little office sound more important than it is. I really don't want to draw a lot of attention to how small we really are.

Dan laughed and then said, "I understand. By the way, don Fernando, I had a long talk yesterday with a lawyer friend of mine back in the States. Remember how, the other day, I was saying that Isaiah Leaf might have gotten away with producing this fake child pornography, this CGI porn, because he wasn't using real children? Well, now I'm not so sure that's true. My attorney friend was of the opinion that if the US government could prove that he was producing pornography that even *looked like* children were involved, they could arrest him."

"Ah, maybe that's why the FBI was interested in him, Dani."

"Maybe," Dan said. "Maybe he wasn't as anonymous as he thought."

*   *   *

The second thing that happened that day that changed Dan's view of the case was that the police spotted Otto Loring and tried to arrest him, but in the ensuing fight, ended up shooting him. This occurred late that evening, many hours after the FBI had left don Fernando's office. In fact, the two FBI agents had already left Panama and were on a flight back to the States.

You may recall that Jorge Manuel had assigned an officer to keep an eye on Melissa's apartment in La Chorrera. Well, late that evening, the officer spotted someone trying to scale the wall around the apartment building. The intruder was dressed in dark clothing and had climbed up the wall and was using a wire cutter to cut through the concertina wire at the top of the wall. The officer was able to grab a leg and pull the person down. The two men scuffled and exchanged blows. At one point, the intruder was able to break away, but instead of running, he grabbed a knife from inside his boot and lunged at the officer. The officer pulled his gun and fired at point-blank range. That stopped the fight. The intruder wasn't killed, but he was gravely injured. It wasn't until he was taken to the hospital that the police realized the intruder was Otto Loring. It was unclear if he would survive, but the police placed a twenty-four-hour guard on him at the hospital.

69

Even though it was past midnight, Jorge Manuel called don Fernando. And of course, don Fernando called Dan to let him know what had happened.

"Has anyone told Melissa Leaf about this?" Dan asked.

"No," don Fernando answered. "We decided not to. The hour is late. Why bother her? Besides, I figured you could tell her tomorrow."

"Me? What are you talking about?" Dan asked.

"You and I can drive to La Chorrera tomorrow and you can tell her," don Fernando said.

"Why do I have to go? Why can't Jorge Manuel tell her?" Dan asked.

"Ah, Dani. I saw the way you looked at her during our interview. This would be a chance to see her again. I will pick you up at eight tomorrow morning."

CHAPTER EIGHT

The next morning, don Fernando picked Dan up at eight o'clock, as he had promised, and they drove to La Chorrera. They stopped by the police station to pick up Jorge Manuel, who was waiting for them outside. Dan suggested that they call Melissa Leaf from the police station, to tell her they were coming over. But don Fernando shook his head no.

"This will just take a minute, Dani. You just need to tell her what happened, then we can leave."

So, Dan turned to Jorge Manuel and asked for the details.

"Officer Antonio Vega was assigned to guard the apartment of Melissa Leaf," Jorge Manuel explained. "He is the one who saw this man climbing the walls surrounding the apartment. There was a terrible fight. Officer Vega received several blows to the head, just like that gringo lawyer did. But when the man pulled a knife, Officer Vega had to shoot him. Officer Vega is a good shot. The bullet narrowly missed the heart. So, we took him to the hospital. They had to operate. The emergency room was very busy, and they had to call a backup surgeon to operate."

"Who did they call?" asked don Fernando.

"They had to call Javier Hugo again," said Jorge Manuel.

"Hmmph," snorted don Fernando. "We certainly are giving that man a lot of business. We should be charging him a fee for the training."

"How did you identify him as Otto Loring?" Dan asked.

"He matched the passport photo that we already had," Jorge Manuel explained. "You know, the photograph that we got from Immigration after that gringo lawyer told Sergeant Sotto that Otto Loring had sent threatening emails to Isaiah Leaf."

"Has anyone interviewed him yet? Dan asked.

"No, señor Landes," Jorge Manuel said. "He has not awoken from the surgery yet."

"Did anyone fingerprint him?" Dan asked.

"Um, no," Jorge Manuel admitted.

"Well, do me a favor and get his prints and confirm his identity. A lot of people look alike in passport photos. You can't be too careful, you know."

"Of course, señor Landes, I will do that," Jorge Manuel said.

Dan was silent for a moment. He thought about what he had just asked Jorge Manuel to do, and then he said to don Fernando, "Don Fernando, can one of you two explain to Melissa Leaf what happened? I would just rather be in the background on this visit."

Don Fernando looked at him and shrugged, but said, "Of course, Dani."

The police car arrived at Melissa Leaf's apartment. Jorge Manuel showed don Fernando and Dan the side of the building where Otto Loring was shot. There was still dried blood on the sidewalk. The three men walked around to the front door and rang Melissa's apartment. She asked who it was through the speaker, then buzzed them upstairs and met them at her apartment door. She seemed shocked to see them.

"Come in, come in," she said. "What can I do for you gentlemen?"

The three men stepped inside. Dan could see that there were several suitcases in the living room off the foyer.

Don Fernando spoke. "We're sorry to bother you, Mrs. Leaf, but we thought you should know that Otto Loring tried to break into this building last night."

Melissa Leaf gasped. Her hand went involuntarily to her mouth. "Oh my God! Did you arrest him?"

"He is under arrest now. He was attempting to climb the wall of your building. When he was confronted, he resisted and attacked one of Captain Jorge Manuel's officers. The officer was forced to shoot him. He is badly wounded and in the hospital now, under police guard. We are not sure if he will survive."

Melissa Leaf's jaw dropped, and the color went out of her face. Her eyes darted left than right. "That's terrible, but... but you caught him and that's good, isn't it? I mean... I... I need to sit down."

"Of course, Mrs. Leaf." Don Fernando gently took her by the arm and guided her into the living room to a large chair.

"Would you like a glass of water?" Dan asked.

"No, no," she replied. "I just need a moment."

"I'll get you some water," Dan said, and walked into the combination dining room and kitchen. He used this as an opportunity to scan the apartment. The suitcases in the living room looked fully packed. The dining room table was covered with file folders and papers. The bedroom was off of the dining room, and Dan could see an open suitcase half-full of clothes on the bed. Melissa Leaf was clearly in the process of packing. He got a glass of water from the kitchen and walked back slowly past the dining room table and tried to read the labels on the file folders. He stepped into the living room and handed the glass of water to Melissa and then sat down across from her.

Don Fernando was in the process of explaining to Melissa exactly what had happened the night before. She was listening, but her eyes were still shifting back and forth, as if she was thinking intently.

When don Fernando finished, she took a sip of the water, managed a half-smile, and said, "I don't know what to say. I mean, it's terrible to think that he was trying to break in... I didn't know him. I didn't even know about him until you told me the other day. But he must have been crazy... If he killed Isaiah... he could have killed me last night. It's all too... too scary."

"Well, it's over now, Mrs. Leaf," don Fernando said. "You don't have to worry anymore. Otto Leaf cannot do you any harm now. If he survives, he will be taken to jail."

Dan watched her eyes, those deep green eyes, moving back and forth, left and right. Finally, he said, "This is one of those cases, Mrs. Leaf, where we are left with two different explanations. On the one hand, we have the official explanation: your husband collapsed suddenly and passed away. The official cause of death is a heart attack. The death certificate was signed by the acting coroner. End of story. In a coincidental, but apparently unrelated event, a disgruntled competitor— Otto Loring—attacked your husband's lawyer and beat him severely. Then that same Otto Loring tried to break into your building and was shot by the police. But those events are unrelated to the death of your husband. And in fact, attacks against tourists fall under the purview of the prosecutors at the Public Ministry in Panama City. So, with that official explanation, our work here is done.

"On the other hand, we have an autopsy that indicates that tetrahydrozoline was found in your late husband's body. Unfortunately, we don't know the amount, and the coroner who did the autopsy still concluded that your husband's death was due to a heart attack. But it *does* lead us to the unofficial speculation that perhaps Otto Loring somehow poisoned your husband. If that's true, and if Mr. Loring survives being shot, he will be charged and convicted for the assault on Mark Handel, and for the attempted burglary last night.

And then he *will be* interrogated by the Public Ministry officials in Panama City. Any attack against a tourist is taken very seriously here in Panama. If he was involved in the death of your husband, I can guarantee you, he will confess. And so, that unofficial speculation may become the official explanation. But even if that does become the official explanation, our investigation here in La Chorrera is still at an end."

Dan paused, then said, "I know that people always want closure when it comes to the death of a loved one. We cannot give you that, at least not right now. And if Mr. Loring does not survive his surgery, we may never know the real truth."

Melissa Leaf nodded and took the last sip of her water.

"I'll put that away for you," Dan said and extended his hand for the glass.

She handed it to him, and he walked back to the kitchen and placed it in the sink. On his way back, he picked up the largest file folder from the dining room table and carried it back with him to the living room.

"I gather you are packing up to leave Panama?" he asked.

"Yes," she said. "It's all been too overwhelming for me. I'm going back to California. I've got family there."

"I understand. I don't blame you a bit. I would do the same thing," Dan said. But then he changed the subject. "I noticed your late husband's medical files on the dining room table," Dan said.

Melissa Leaf nodded. "Yes," she said, "I wasn't sure what to do with them."

"One of the things that bothered me," Dan said, "that made me think that Otto Loring did somehow murder your husband was the fact that your husband had no history of heart problems... or at least, I think that's what you told Sergeant Sotto."

"If Isaiah did, he never told *me*," Melissa said.

"May I just have a look at this?" Dan asked.

"Of course."

Dan leafed through the file, looking at the different charts and reports. He stopped on one page and read for a bit, then closed the file.

"It's all medical terminology to me," he said and smiled. He placed the file on a small table next to his chair. "We've taken up too much of your time, Mrs. Leaf. We'll be going now. Do you know when you're leaving?"

"We haven't bought our tickets yet."

"We?" Dan asked.

"Oh... well, Mr. Handel wanted to go back to California, too. He's got some business there, so he agreed to help me get home."

"Ah, that was kind of him," Dan said. "Well, good luck."

Dan stood up, gestured to don Fernando and Jorge Manuel, and all three men left.

When they got inside don Fernando's police car, Dan turned to don Fernando. "Can you call Immigration and flag both Melissa Leaf's and Mark Handel's passports, so we know when they leave Panama?

"Of course, Dani," don Fernando said.

Then turning to Jorge Manuel, Dan said, "I would like to talk with this Dr. Javier Hugo. Can you arrange that?"

"Sí, señor," Jorge Manuel replied.

"Something bothering you, Dani?" don Fernando asked.

"Yeah, but I don't quite know what it is," Dan replied. "But something's been nagging at me ever since those two FBI agents showed up. I just can't quite put my finger on it."

Jorge Manuel got on his cell phone and called Sergeant Sotto and asked him if he could arrange for the three men to stop by the La Chorrera Hospital to visit Dr. Hugo. Don Fernando started the car and headed for the La Chorrera police department, but a few minutes later, Jorge Manuel's cell phone rang. It was Sergeant Sotto calling to say that Dr. Hugo could see the three men now. So, don Fernando changed direction for the La Chorrera Hospital.

Once there, the three men found Dr. Hugo in his office on the third floor. After Jorge Manuel introduced his two companions and made apologies for their sudden visit, Dan launched into his questions.

"I understand that you did the surgery on that man who was shot in the chest last night, the one that the police are now guarding."

Dr. Hugo nodded yes.

"What do you think his chances of surviving are?" Dan asked.

Dr. Hugo shrugged. "The bullet was very close to his heart," he said. "I did the best I could do. In matters like this, we have to trust in God."

"I see," said Dan. "But do you have an opinion as to his chances?"

Dr Hugo shrugged again. "Only God knows."

"O-kay," Dan said slowly. "Well, let me ask you this: you were at the hospital when the body of Isaiah Leaf arrived, right?"

"Si, señor."

"And his wife was with him, correct?"

"Yes, that is true. The emergency room attendants were performing CPR on the man, but it was obviously too late. I talked to the woman in the hallway and tried to break the news to her gently."

"And you were there because you were the emergency room doctor?" Dan asked.

"It was a busy night. I am one of the backup physicians. They called me in."

"But you also performed the autopsy?" Dan asked.

"Yes, Capitán Manuel asked me to," Dr. Hugo said.

"But you're not the regular coroner?"

"No, I am just a backup coroner."

"And do you have any formal training in doing autopsies?" Dan asked.

Dr. Hugo looked a little stressed by the question. He shrugged and said, "Well, I went to medical school..."

"I see," said Dan. "Well, tell me, why did you use a Conklin Toxicology test?"

"Well... Capitán Manuel seemed to imply that he wasn't sure that the man's death was natural."

"But why the Conklin test? Why *that* test and not a complete toxicology profile, that would have told you the quantity of drugs in the man's body?"

Dr. Hugo bit his lip. He glanced at Jorge Manuel and then said, "Well, I knew that the police department didn't have a large budget for these kinds of extra autopsies... I mean, they could have called in a more experienced coroner from Panama City, but that would have cost a lot more money, so I figured that..."

His voice trailed off. Dan nodded and said, "I understand. Okay, so the Conklin Test came back positive for marijuana and tetrahydrozoline, right?"

Dr. Hugo nodded. He obviously was not used to being cross-examined like this, and was very uncomfortable, but since Jorge Manuel and don Fernando were both standing there permitting Dan to question him in this manner, there was nothing he could do.

"So, when you saw the tetrahydrozoline, why didn't you order a specific exam to establish the blood level for just the tetrahydrozoline?" Dan asked.

"Well, um," Dr. Hugo stammered. "I... I looked it up and, um... it wasn't a narcotic. So, I didn't think it was important."

Dan finally understood, and so he said softly, "You didn't know what it was, did you?"

Dr. Hugo made an apologetic shrug.

Dan nodded and was quiet for a minute.

Then Dr. Hugo said, "I had never heard of this drug before. So I looked it up and put it in my report. I thought if it was important, the police would order more tests later."

"But the body was cremated the next day, right?" Dan said.

"Well, yes it was."

"So how could the police department order more tests?" Dan asked.

"Well, I kept a vial of blood."

Dan's jaw dropped. "What?"

"I kept one vial of blood in case the police wanted to pay for more tests."

Dan's heart started pounding fast. "And you still have that vial of blood?"

"Yes, of course."

"Can you send it immediately to a toxicology lab for a complete—and I mean *complete*—analysis?" Dan asked. Then he added, "The cost doesn't matter." He glanced over at Jorge Manuel who nodded in agreement.

"Yes, of course. I will do that immediately. It should be ready by tomorrow."

"Can you call us the moment that report is complete?" Dan said.

"Yes, of course."

Jorge Manuel spoke up. "I will have one of my men pick the report up as soon as it is ready."

"Dr. Hugo, I want to thank you," Dan said. "I apologize for my questions. But thank God you had the foresight to save a vial of blood."

Dan took Dr. Hugo's hand and shook it vigorously.

Dr. Hugo smiled broadly. He had somehow managed to save himself, and was much relieved.

CHAPTER NINE

The next afternoon, don Fernando called Dan to tell him that Jorge Manuel had just arrived in Villa Rosario with the toxicology report. Dan hurried down to the police station.

Dan wasn't sure exactly what he was looking for. In police work, as in life, one often asks questions not knowing what the answer is going to be. He just knew that something had been gnawing at him ever since his first interview with Melissa Leaf. He had asked for the toxicology report partly because he wanted to know how much tetrahydrozoline was in the dead man's body, but also because he was searching for an answer to a question that he couldn't even form yet.

Jorge Manuel handed Dan the report. It was several pages long. Dan sat down and read it carefully while the other two men sat and waited patiently.

"Ah," Dan said, pointing to a line at the bottom of the first page and holding up the report so that both don Fernando and Jorge Manuel could see. "You see here where it says that the amount of tetrahydrozoline was 140 ng/ml? That's nanograms to milliliter, as in 140 nanograms of tetrahydrozoline in a milliliter of blood. If I remember correctly from my detective days, a lethal dose of tetrahydrozoline is anything over sixty or seventy nanograms, so... *that's* what killed him."

"So, he definitely was murdered?" Jorge Manuel asked.

"Well... I can't say that," Dan replied. "I can say that the tetrahydrozoline induced the heart attack, but how that drug got into his system, we still don't know. But this certainly makes it more probable that he was murdered."

Dan turned the report around and continued reading. He turned to the second page, but then he stopped.

"Oh my God," he said softly.

He started off into space. "Fuck me," he said. "Now it all makes sense."

Don Fernando and Jorge Manuel looked at each other.

"What is it, Dani?" don Fernando asked.

Dan handed the report to don Fernando.

"The dead man's blood type was A-positive."

Don Fernando shrugged and asked, "So?"

Dan took a deep breath and said, "When I was reading Isaiah Leaf's medical reports yesterday in Melissa's apartment, I noticed that his blood type was O-positive. I noticed it because it's the same as mine."

Don Fernando and Jorge Manuel just stared at Dan, waiting for him to explain more.

"Don't you see, guys? The man on the autopsy table wasn't Isaiah Leaf!" Dan said. "It was somebody else! I *knew* something wasn't right! His wife said he never drank or took drugs, but the autopsy report showed marijuana. At first, I just chalked it up to her not knowing her husband well, but it *bothered* me. Then there was the fact that Dr. Hugo never did an independent ID on the body. Melissa Leaf just told the hospital it was her husband, and everyone just believed her. Then she had the body cremated right away. Fuck me! They faked his death!"

Jorge Manuel looked confused. "So, Isaiah Leaf wasn't murdered?"

"No, but *somebody* was. They had to have found someone who looked similar, but not someone who was well-known. It had to be a gringo, about the same age... but somebody traveling alone, so if he disappeared, he wouldn't be missed."

Don Fernando asked, "You think the wife did this?".

"I think both Melissa Leaf and Isaiah Leaf conspired to do this. As for Mark Handel... I don't know, but my hunch is that he was also involved."

"What about this Otto Loring?" Jorge Manuel asked.

Dan paused. "I don't know where he fits in," he finally said.

Don Fernando spoke again. "And if Isaiah Leaf is not dead, where is he?"

"That's another good question," Dan said and frowned. "You know, this may sound kind of stupid, but can you call Immigration and see if someone using Isaiah Leaf's passport has left the country? I don't think he'd be that dumb, but you never know."

"Of course, Dani."

Don Fernando picked up his phone and started dialing.

"I still don't understand, don Landes," Jorge Manuel said. "Why would señor Leaf and his wife do this? They had a good marriage; they had plenty of money; what would they gain from taking this enormous risk?"

"Anonymity, Jorge Manuel, anonymity. What was the one thing that Isaiah Leaf and Mark Handel both did consistently? *They protected themselves*. They put layers and layers of shell companies between the person Isaiah Leaf and the pornography he was creating. No one even knew what Isaiah Leaf looked like, and yet... and yet, the FBI was hot on his trail. And maybe he got wind of that. Well, what better protection than if the world thinks you're dead? Especially if you're about to start selling child pornography on the dark web. Mark Handel is a smart lawyer. He would have figured out that the fact that Isaiah was creating CGI children on his computer rather than using real children wouldn't give him any legal protection. Half the countries in the world could arrest him if they could prove he was creating child porn. But not if the world believed he was dead. He could produce child porn for a couple of years, make a few billion dollars, and then just evaporate into the ultra-rich circles of Dubai, Bulgaria, or Monaco."

Jorge Manuel just shook his head and said, "It just seems so crazy."

"Money is a drug," Dan replied. "It's very addictive. The more you get, the more you want. Plus, Isaiah probably liked the adrenaline rush from doing something illegal. I mean, look at the business he was in. Money for nothing, as they say. He was making millions, but if the world thought he was dead, he could make *billions*."

Don Fernando finished talking on the phone and hung it up. "Bad news, Dani. Nobody using Isaiah Leaf's passport has left the country."

"Well, that's not bad news," Dan said.

"No, Dani, the bad news is that both Melissa Leaf and Mark Handel *have* left Panama. They flew out on the same flight this morning."

"Fuck me!" Dan exclaimed. "Do you know where they went?"

"San José,"

"Hmm, well, Melissa did say she and Mark Handel were going back to California," Dan mused.

"No, Dani, San José, Costa Rica."

"They just flew next door to Costa Rica?!" Dan asked incredulously.

Don Fernando nodded his head and shrugged. "It's just a ninety-minute flight from Panama City," he said. "But that might not be their final destination. From San José, they could fly anywhere in the world. I asked Immigration to check with the Costa Rican authorities to see if they took a connecting flight anywhere else."

Dan thought for a moment, then said. "No, you're right. They could be going anywhere."

Jorge Manuel spoke up. "Have they done the perfect crime, señor Landes? I mean, we can't issue a warrant for them for the murder of Isaiah Leaf if Isaiah Leaf is still alive. And we can't issue a warrant for the murder of the dead man that Javier Hugo did the autopsy on—we don't know who he was, and we don't have a body. There's no real evidence that a murder was even committed. How could they be prosecuted?"

"True," said Dan, "but they *could be* prosecuted for insurance fraud. Both Melissa Leaf and Mark Handel filed life insurance claims. If we could prove that Isaiah Leaf was still alive, then they could be prosecuted for fraud."

Don Fernando shook his head. "I don't know, Dani. Panama doesn't have a very good history of prosecuting fraud—or any white-collar crime, for that matter—and neither Koke or I have the budget to go searching for these people outside of Panama."

"No, you don't," agreed Dan, "but the two insurance companies that issued those life insurance policies *do have* those resources. Plus, they have the motivation. They don't want to pay out millions of dollars in benefits if they don't have to. Jorge Manuel, that sergeant of yours has talked to both those insurance companies, right?"

Jorge Manuel nodded yes.

"Can you have him contact those companies again, and tell them... well, hmm, there's not much to tell them, is there? Well, he can say that we have discovered a discrepancy in the blood type of the individual that died and the medical records of Isaiah Leaf, and we have a suspicion that the person who died was *not* Isaiah Leaf, and that there might be some insurance fraud going on... Yeah, just have your sergeant tell them that, and we can see how they respond. If I know insurance companies, they will jump on that."

Jorge Manuel nodded and took out his cell phone and began dialing Sergeant Sotto's number.

Dan turned to don Fernando and said, "In the meantime, don Fernando, let's try to coordinate with Costa Rican Immigration and track wherever Melissa and Mark Handel go next. We need to keep tabs on them." Dan paused then added, "You know, we're probably going to have to contact the FBI and tell those two agents what we've discovered."

"Oh damnit! Dani. I was afraid you were going to say that," don Fernando said. "Do I have to tell them about the autopsy?"

"Hmm, maybe not," Dan replied. "You could just say we just discovered that the attending physician in the ER took a blood sample, and that, um, *because of the FBI's inquiry,* we decided to have it analyzed. I mean, that's kind of true. After all, Javier Hugo was one of the physicians in the ER the night the ambulance brought the body to the ER. You can make the agents feel that they were somehow responsible for this new development."

Don Fernando nodded. "Yes, Dani, that is a good idea, but let me ask you this. Is there any point in involving the FBI if the insurance companies are not interested in pursuing this case?"

"Oh, I think the insurance companies will be interested."

"Well, let's see how they react, and if they are interested, *then* I will call the FBI."

Dan smiled and said, "That's fine."

CHAPTER TEN

As fate would have it, at the exact moment that Dan, don Fernando, and Jorge Manuel were in don Fernando's office discussing the toxicology report, Melissa Leaf was sharing a coffee with Mark Handel in a quiet café in San José, Costa Rica.

"What time did he say he was coming," Melissa asked, with a hint of nervousness in her voice.

Mark looked at his watch. "He should be here any time now," he said. "Relax, Melissa. Everything is going perfectly. It's a beautiful day; we're in a beautiful country; and as soon as the insurance companies deposit our money, we'll be beautiful multi-millionaires. Speaking of beautifully, you played those cops in Panama perfectly."

"They scared the shit out of me when they showed up suddenly at the condo. Fuck, I thought they were going to arrest me. That fucking Otto Loring almost screwed everything up."

"To the contrary, Melissa," Mark said. "Otto Loring was a godsend. The police think he killed that... that... what was his name?"

"Glen... Glen Hartz..." Melissa said softly.

"Yeah," continued Mark. "The police will think that Otto killed Glen Hartz. Otto gave us the perfect alibi. We should thank our lucky stars. Good luck like that only happens once in a lifetime."

Melissa stirred her coffee. "I don't think I'll be able to relax until we get to Spain," she said.

Mark patted her arm. "I understand," he said. "But we need to hang out here for maybe a week. I've been pressuring the insurance companies to pay up, threatening to sue them. We should have our money in six or seven days. Then we can convert it to crypto and be gone."

Melissa nodded. "I just hate the waiting," she said.

"I know," Mark replied.

Just then, Isaiah Leaf walked up to the table. Melissa jumped up and hugged him tight and gave him a big kiss.

"Oh, Isaiah, I've missed you so much," she said.

Isaiah hugged her back. "Me too," he said, then said, "but you will have to learn to not call me Isaiah in public. You'll have to start calling me Glen."

"Oh, that's so creepy," Melissa said.

"You're still using Glen's passport?" Mark asked.

"I'm having new ones made in Madrid," said Isaiah. "They'll be ready when we arrive." You're both getting new ones, too. But for the moment, you two have to use your old ones, and I'll use Glen's. It's so much more complicated these days to get new passports. They have these chips in them that have to be carefully programmed with new identities and new travel histories. It takes time. But my guys in Madrid are the best. As soon as we land in Madrid, we can leave our old lives behind forever. It's so exciting!"

The waiter came over to their table. Isaiah ordered a cup of coffee.

"Okay," Isaiah said after the waiter brought his coffee. "Fill me in on exactly what happened in Panama."

"It was so scary," Melissa said, holding onto Isaiah's arm. "I thought for sure we were going to get caught."

"Nah," Mark interrupted. "Everything went great. The police were so stupid. It was like taking candy from a baby."

"Well, tell me the details," Isaiah said.

"Okay," said Mark. "After we put Glen's body at your desk, and after you and I left, Melissa called 911. The ambulance came and the two attendants tried to do CPR on Glen. But of course... it was too late. Anyway, Melissa rode in the ambulance to the hospital. She did a great job of acting all hysterical. She had the doctor call me, and I came to the hospital and we both told the doctors it was you..."

"But then the next day, they did an autopsy," blurted out Melissa.

"Really?" said Isaiah and frowned. "Why?"

"The doctor said it was standard procedure," said Melissa.

"But it didn't prove anything," added Mark. "The death certificate said heart attack."

"But then, the police called me in for an interview and said there were those eyedrops in Glen's body."

Mark made a dismissive motion with his hand. "Still, nothing was proved. They only know that the chemical was in his body; they didn't know how much; and they ended up admitting that the official cause of death was still natural, still a heart attack. And the insurance companies didn't ask any questions when I sent them the death certificate."

"Okay, good," said Isaiah.

Mark continued talking. "Then that fucker Otto Loring showed up out of the blue and attacked me one night outside a bar! I thought we had made it clear to him last month that he was out of our deal. That asshole, he totally blindsided me. I ended up going to the hospital and got six stitches."

"Yeah, I see the scar. Looks painful," Isaiah said.

"It still hurts. I was so pissed, but... it turned out to be a blessing in disguise, because it made the police think that he killed you... I mean, killed Glen. And *then*, he tried to break into your condo two nights ago, and the police fucking *shot* him! It was so great! He's under police guard at the hospital, but the police told Melissa yesterday that he may not survive. And if he does survive, he's going to jail. I mean, things could not have worked out more perfectly! Now that Otto is under arrest, the police have closed the case. We're totally in the clear. Things couldn't be better."

CHAPTER ELEVEN

Dan was correct in his prediction. The insurance companies were not just interested in his theory that Isaiah was not dead—they were *very* interested. Thus, the next day, don Fernando got a call from one Mitch Rivera, a fraud investigator from the Unilateral Insurance Company. Mark Handel and Melissa Leaf had taken out different life insurance policies on Isaiah Leaf through different insurance companies in different states, but as fate would have it, both of those companies were actually owned by the Unilateral Insurance Company. Unilateral was looking at a combined payout of twenty-five million dollars for Isaiah's death, so Unilateral put one of their top fraud investigators—Mitch Rivera—on a plane to Panama the very next day. Mitch was known for being rigorous in his methods, bordering on obsessive, but he did speak Spanish, and he had an excellent track record in uncovering insurance fraud.

And so it was that a few days later, Dan found himself sitting once again in a conference room in don Fernando's police station along with don Fernando, Jorge Manuel, and a very well-organized Mitch Rivera.

Mitch took two pencils and a pen from his leather briefcase and aligned them next to each other on the conference table. Then he took out several typed pages and placed them very exactly next to the two pencils. "I interviewed your Sergeant Sotto this morning," he said, "and these are my typed notes. I must commend Sergeant Sotto's excellent memory. He could almost recite his interviews with Mrs. Leaf and Mr. Handel from memory. Quite remarkable.

I would like to have a man like that on our staff. He was able to provide me with a wealth of material on these two suspects."

"So, you think the lawyer was part of this crime?" Jorge Manuel asked.

"Undoubtedly," said Mitch.

Dan spoke up. "You realize that this whole case rests on the blood types being different? I mean, if the toxicology lab in Panama City made an error, or if there was a typo on the medical reports that I saw..."

Mitch smiled and shook his head no. "No," he said. "As part of the insurance application, Mrs. Leaf had to give us access to Isaiah Leaf's medical records. We checked them carefully. And I had the toxicology lab in Panama City retest the blood for blood type. I can say conclusively that the man on the autopsy table was *not* Isaiah Leaf."

"But is the difference in blood types enough to get a conviction for insurance fraud?" Dan asked.

"No, not by itself," agreed Mitch. "To prove insurance fraud, we need collateral corroborating evidence. But the difference in blood type is enough for us to deny the claim. And that shifts the burden to them. If they want their money, they will have to sue us, and then *they* have to prove that it was Isaiah Leaf who died... and of course, they won't be able to do that. For small fraud claims, for example, when someone overestimates the value of something that was damaged in a fire, we usually just deny the claim and the perpetrator just goes away. But for something of this scale, we always try and prosecute."

Dan nodded. Then he turned to don Fernando and asked, "Have you notified the FBI?"

Don Fernando pursed his lips and said, "Yes, Dani. I had a long talk with FBI agent Ian Williams the other day. I explained how their visit caused us to investigate further, and then how we discovered that there was that drug in the dead man's body and the issue with the blood type. Then I put them in contact with señor Rivera."

"Yes," Mitch said. "Agent Williams and I have had several conversations. I guess they are interested in this Isaiah Leaf for other reasons, but we have agreed to join forces."

"Good," said Dan. "But back to proving insurance fraud. How would you do that?"

"Ideally, we'd like a confession and proof of who the deceased was, neither of which we have right now. So, we have to build our case. First, we have to keep track of them. These are people of means. If they disappear into Europe, it becomes very difficult for us. So, we have two investigators in Costa Rica right now, who are tailing them. We've identified the hotel where Melissa Leaf and Mark Handel are staying, but so far, we've been unable to determine where Isaiah Leaf is staying. So that's an issue. Once we can locate him, the next thing we want is a photograph of Isaiah Leaf together with his wife and Mark Handel. If we had a good photograph of them together, that would be enough to take to a grand jury in the United States. The insurance applications prove that both his wife and his lawyer took out life insurance on him; the claim for benefits that each of them filed has their signed statements that Isaiah passed away; the blood test proves Isaiah Leaf is not the dead man; and the photographs would prove that both his wife and his lawyer knew he was still alive yet persisted in their insurance claim. So, to that end, we have two of our undercover photographers in Costa Rica working with our two investigators."

"Wow," said Dan, "so you've got four people in San José right now? That's amazing."

"Well, five people, if you count FBI agent Brian Dickerson. Agent Williams sent his partner to San José yesterday to work with our two investigators."

Dan nodded his approval. "I'm impressed by your rapid response," he said.

Mitch shrugged and said, "Twenty-five million dollars is a lot of money. We at Unilateral take great umbrage at this type of fraud."

"Well, it sounds like you've got things under control. Is there anything you need from us?" Dan asked.

"There is the issue of who the dead man was. Your Immigration office says that no one has filed a missing persons report on anyone who would match the height, weight, and age description of the body that was brought to the hospital. Immigration also tells me that no one matching that description has overstayed their visa. So, it's a waiting game. If it was a random tourist they befriended, his visa would have to run out before Immigration would notice him, and that could be up to six months from now. So, we could use some help in this area. If your police officers could check every hotel in La Chorrera, it would be of great assistance."

Mitch Rivera reached into his briefcase. "I've got copies of a general description we've put together. We're looking for a solo traveler who matches this description who recently stayed at one of your hotels... maybe he recently checked out, or maybe left without paying and left items behind."

Jorge Manuel took the papers from Mitch and read the description.

"It's not much of a description, I know," Mitch said. "But it's all we got."

Jorge Manuel nodded and said, "We will do our best."

"Have you notified them yet that their claims are being denied?" Dan asked.

"Not yet," Mitch said. "The timing of that is rather tricky. Normally we would send a very short email that says something like 'after careful investigation your claim is being denied, and if you have any questions, please contact our fraud investigation unit,' but in this case, we don't want to spook them, so we're not sending them anything. We're afraid they will bolt. So, we're just going to give them the silent treatment until we can get a photograph of Isaiah Leaf with at least one of the other two. Every time they ask about their money, we will just reply that the claim is under review. Right now, it's just a waiting game. We're waiting to get a photograph or get a lead on the dead guy... just waiting to catch a break.”

CHAPTER TWELVE

Mark Handel's cell phone rang. He looked at his caller ID. It was the number of Isaiah's new burner phone. Mark's chest tightened. He knew what was coming. Nonetheless, he answered it.

"Hello."

"What the fuck is going on with the insurance companies?!" Isaiah barked.

"I don't know, boss," Mark said. "They keep giving me the runaround."

"You told me they would pay up last *week*!" Isaiah said.

"They should have!" replied Mark. "It's in their contract. I keep threatening to sue them for violating their own terms, but they just keep saying they're reviewing the claim."

This is bullshit!" Isaiah said. "The only reason we're sitting in this shithole country is to have easy access to our US accounts. What's the point of staying here if they're fucking with our money? We should get our asses to Europe... now!"

"We could do that if you want. But Melissa and I will have to fly back to the States once they pay us. We can't liquidate that much money without making at least one personal appearance."

Isaiah was silent for a moment. Then he said. "I don't like this. Something is fucked up. The other day I could have sworn someone was following me. What are the chances they're on to us?"

"Zero, boss. Absolutely zero. How *could* they be? We haven't done anything wrong. We've got a certified death certificate. We had a valid insurance policy. The insurance companies are just being dicks."

The line was silent again. Then Isaiah said, "Okay, here's what we're going to do. First, I want you to fly to the States and file lawsuits against the insurance companies to crank up the pressure. Second, I'm going to Spain. I just have a bad feeling about staying here in Costa Rica. Something doesn't feel right. I'll ask Melissa what she wants to do. She can come with me to Spain or go with you to the States."

"Whatever you say, boss."

*   *   *

At the same time that Isaiah was having this rather one-way conversation with Mark Handel, don Fernando was on the phone with Dan Landes.

"Ah, Dani... I just got off the phone with my new best friend, Ian Williams." Don Fernando said.

"Oh? He's your new best friend now?"

"Yes, Dani. I was explaining to him how much we need a crypto expert. Our tech guy is good, but he's only good at hacking into computers and cell phones. We need someone who can help us track cryptocurrency money laundering. Señor Williams is going to help me apply for another FBI grant."

"I see," said Dan. "Well, congratulations."

"But that is not why I called, Dani. I called to tell you that señor Williams told me that the insurance people in Costa Rica got a photograph of Isaiah Leaf talking with his wife. Señor Williams is very happy. He said that they are going to show the picture to some big jury in the United States."

"Ah... that would be a grand jury," said Dan. "Well, that's good, don Fernando. That's how they will get an indictment, and then they can arrest him."

"Yes, señor Williams was explaining that to me. I do not understand your legal system, Dani. Here, we arrest the criminal first and then we take them in front of a judge, but

98

in *your* country, you go in front of a jury first, and then you arrest them. It seems backwards to me."

Dan laughed. "Yeah, well, the US is strange. But basically, the grand jury is just a way to get an arrest warrant. It's a way for the government to test their evidence. But anyway, this is progress. So maybe they will arrest those folks in Costa Rica and extradite them back to the US."

"I think so, Dani. Señor Williams told me that was his plan. I asked him to keep us informed. Maybe the FBI will pay for us to go the United States and testify."

"Oh, I doubt that, don Fernando. They don't need us to make this case."

*   *   *

But, as fate would have it, things did not go according to FBI agent Williams's plan. Agent Williams took the photograph of Isaiah and Melissa to the grand jury and got fraud indictments against both of them. But he couldn't get an indictment against Mark Handel, because he didn't have a photograph of Isaiah *with* Mark, so he didn't have any proof that Mark knew that Isaiah was alive. Because of this, Agent Williams did not start the arrest procedures against Isaiah and Melissa. He wanted to wait until he could get a photograph of Isaiah and Mark together so that he could arrest all three co-conspirators at the same time. Unfortunately for him, this delay gave Isaiah and Melissa just enough time to leave Costa Rica. They both flew to Madrid. Melissa used her own passport and Isaiah used Glen Hartz's passport. Because there was no arrest warrant out for either of them, they were able to pass through Immigration in both Costa Rica and Spain. Once they got to Madrid, Isaiah picked up his and Melissa's new passports and identity cards from his counterfeiter contact, and he and Melissa changed their identities. Mark left Costa Rica for the United States, as Isaiah had directed him to do. He filed a lawsuit against the insurance companies for both his and Melissa's benefits. The

Unilateral Insurance company, which owned both insurance companies, was required to file an answer to Mark's lawsuit. So they did, and they alleged fraud. That tipped off Mark that the jig was up. Isaiah shipped a new passport and identity cards to Mark via FedEx, and using his new passport, Mark was able to fly out of the United States and join Isaiah and Melissa in Madrid. Both the FBI and Unilateral Insurance investigators lost their trail. And Isaiah, Melissa and Mark Handel simply evaporated into Europe. Agent Williams sent a request to Interpol for an international warrant, or as it is known, a red notice. But Interpol has strict guidelines for international warrants, and when they looked at an alleged criminal insurance fraud case, that was based on a single photograph, they declined to issue a red notice for Isaiah and Melissa Leaf.

Thus, it was a bad week for both FBI Agent Williams and Unilateral Insurance Fraud Investigator Mitch Rivera. Mitch Rivera took the bad news in stride. He had hoped for the rapid arrest of Isaiah and Melissa Leaf and Mark Handel. Nonetheless, he had succeeded in his primary mission of protecting Unilateral Insurance from having to pay the insurance claim. Because Mark Handel had fled to Europe, he failed to pursue the lawsuit he filed, and the court eventually dismissed it. Mitch Rivera was satisfied with the result.

FBI Agent Ian Williams, on the other hand, took the recent news rather hard, mostly of course, because it was *his fault* that he had not acted more quickly in arresting Isaiah and Melissa Leaf. It was a personal defeat for him, and he was determined to track them down.

However, don Fernando was able to give agent Williams a bit of good news. When Agent Williams told don Fernando that Melissa Leaf had flown from San José, Costa Rica, to Madrid, Spain, don Fernando suggested that perhaps Isaiah Leaf had flown on that same airplane with her, but under a different name. Don Fernando was able to get a passenger list for that flight from the Costa Rican Immigration and was able to match up those names and passport numbers with visitors to Panama, and more specifically, with visitors to the city of La Chorrera. A man named Glen Hartz had been staying in La Chorrera at the same time as Isaiah and Melissa Leaf had lived there. That man happened to have the same age, height, and weight as Isaiah Leaf. He had checked out of his hotel two nights before Melissa called 911 to report her husband's heart attack. Furthermore, someone using Glen Hartz's passport had flown from Panama to Costa Rica on the same airplane as Melissa Leaf and Mark Handel. Don Fernando was able to get a copy of Glen Hartz's passport photograph from the US Embassy in Panama, and he showed it to Dr. Javier Hugo. Dr. Hugo identified that as the man whose autopsy he had done.

Based on this evidence, don Fernando was able to convince the prosecutor's office in Panama City to issue arrest warrants for Isaiah and Melissa Leaf for the murder of Glen Hartz. However, when Interpol looked at the evidence underlying this arrest warrant—which was admittedly all circumstantial—Interpol once again declined to issue a red notice.

Nonetheless, Agent Williams was grateful for don Fernando's help in identifying the murder victim, and thus—totally coincidently—the FBI approved don Fernando's grant request for money to hire a new crypto expert for his police department.

Of course, no one knew that Isaiah, Melissa, and Mark Handel all had new identities. With new identities, and without an Interpol red notice for their arrest, the threesome was able to move freely anywhere in Europe—which they did. Isaiah was working hard on perfecting his new CGI child porn for the dark web, but he could do that work anywhere there was Wi-Fi. He didn't know the details of how the insurance company knew that he had faked his own death. But the fact that they *did* know made him very skittish. He insisted that the three of them change their location every few weeks.

As time went on, Agent Williams became more determined to catch Isaiah and Melissa Leaf and, if possible, Mark Handel. Then, something happened that gave him a new idea.

CHAPTER THIRTEEN

Several weeks passed by with no breaks in the case. But there came a day when don Fernando had to call Agent Williams with some bad news. He didn't want to do it, but he felt he had no choice. He knew that Agent Williams was utterly convinced that Isaiah Leaf, his wife, and Mark Handel were responsible for the murder of Glen Hartz. But don Fernando thought that maybe the reason that Agent Williams was so convinced was because those three suspects had escaped his grasp. Don Fernando had noticed in previous conversations that Agent Williams never liked to talk about Otto Loring, and specifically that Agent Williams got very uncomfortable, and even angry, if anyone brought up the possibility that Otto Loring might have murdered Glen Hartz. Nonetheless, don Fernando had news about Otto Loring that had to be conveyed to Agent Williams. And so, after thinking about his options, don Fernando asked Dan to make the call for him. After all, there was no point in jeopardizing his relationship with such a fine benefactor as Agent Williams over bad news that could be delivered by someone else. And so, Dan made the call to the FBI agent, and after a few pleasantries, got to the point.

"Agent Williams, the reason for this call is to give you an update on this case. You remember Otto Loring, the man the police shot outside of Melissa Leaf's apartment building?"

"Yes?"

"Well, he's still in the hospital, but the doctors are saying that he has recovered enough that they will want to release him sometime this week," Dan explained.

"Okay, so?

"Well, when he's released from the hospital, he'll be free to go. The prosecutor is not going to press charges against him," Dan said.

"What?! Why not?"

"Because there is a fundamental difference in the law down here in Panama versus the United States," Dan explained. Panamanian law is based on the Napoleonic Code. A person cannot be prosecuted down here unless there is a complaining witness. Since both Mark Handel and Melissa Leaf have left the country and not filed a criminal complaint, the prosecutor can't charge Otto Loring with any crime."

"What about the police officer that shot him? He saw Otto Loring trying to climb into Melissa Leaf's building," Agent Williams sputtered.

"The police officer is a corroborating witness, but the prosecutor still needs a complaining witness. Down here, the victim must file an official complaint in order for a case to proceed."

"That's ridiculous!" snapped Agent Williams.

"Well, that's Panama... and every other country in Central and South America," said Dan. "I know this doesn't affect your case, but don Fernando wanted to keep you updated."

The line was silent for a moment, then Agent Williams said, "You know, maybe this can help us... When is Loring supposed to be released?"

"The end of the week, probably Thursday or Friday," Dan said.

"Is he still under guard at the hospital?"

"Yes, but that will end when the doctors release him," Dan explained.

The line was silent again. Another thirty seconds went by. Dan wondered if he had lost the connection.

"Are you still there?" Dan asked.

"Yes, yes, I'm thinking," Agent Williams said. "Okay, look, I'm coming down to see this guy. I'll fly down tomorrow morning. I'm going to need your help. Don't let him get released before I get there. Does this guy speak English?"

"Oh yes, he speaks German and English. His Spanish is actually pretty bad."

"Okay, well I'm still going to need your help. Let me make some plane reservations and I'll call you back."

And thus it came to pass that Agent Williams returned to Panama. The very next afternoon, he was at the Villa Rosario police station explaining his idea to don Fernando, Dan, and Jorge Manuel.

"As you know, we had hoped to arrest Isaiah Leaf, his wife, and Mark Handel last month in Costa Rica for insurance fraud, but they slipped away from us and fled to Europe. And the fact is, gentlemen, that the trail has gone cold. The FBI has no jurisdiction in Europe, and Interpol has been less than cooperative. I know that I was less than candid with you the last time I was here about why the FBI is so interested in Mr. Leaf, but I can tell you more now."

Agent Williams paused to gather his thoughts, in the way that someone gathers their thoughts when they want to tell you something without telling you everything.

"Mr. Leaf has been on our radar for quite some time. He is very active in the worldwide distribution of adult pornography. This is an area of criminality that the FBI takes very seriously. We consider it part of our mission to track down and arrest all those engaged in the production and distribution of illegal pornography. I have been a part of the FBI's Anti-pornography Task Force for the past five years, and we've been tracking Mr. Leaf all that time. Unfortunately, we've never been able to arrest him because he—with the help of his lawyer—has been very clever about staying just within the boundaries of what separates legal and illegal pornography. By staying just inside those limits, he has managed to become the most prolific producer of pornography that the FBI has ever seen. That is why, when we heard, two months ago, that he had supposedly died, we came down here to be sure. Our suspicions were correct, and as we now all know, of course, he faked his own death in an effort to stay one step ahead of the law."

Dan tried to maintain a concerned and interested facial expression as Agent Williams talked. He nodded at appropriate times, but he couldn't help but wonder: If Agent Williams was admitting that Isaiah Leaf hadn't done anything illegal in the five years that the FBI was tracking him, why did they want to arrest him? But Dan knew better than to ask obvious questions to an FBI agent.

"Recently," Agent Williams continued, "I became a member of the VCACITF, the Violent Crimes Against Children International Task Force. We have information that Mr. Leaf is planning to produce child pornography to market on the dark web. Stopping him has become the number one priority of our task force.

"But, to be honest, prosecuting pornography cases is a time-consuming and risky endeavor. We don't always get the convictions that we should. But, thanks to the efforts of your fine police captain Jose Fernando here, we might have the chance to prosecute Isaiah Leaf for the federal crime of insurance fraud, a charge that is considerably easier to prove. Unfortunately, he has evaded our agents and disappeared into Europe, and as I stated, the trail has gone cold. That is where Otto Loring becomes important."

Dan felt his heart rate increase. Now we're getting somewhere, he told himself.

"Otto Loring is a small fish in the world of pornography," Agent Williams said. "He likes to think he's a major player, but he's not. He's more of a pimp. He manages a stable of young actors and actresses in Europe and, for a fee, helps connect them with pornography directors. He also produces his own pornography DVD films for distribution in Europe. Normally, he would not be of interest to the FBI, but he *does know* a lot of people; he moves in the pornography circles; he's well known in the pornography world.

"So, what I would like to do, gentlemen—and I would need your help with this—is I would like to convince Otto Loring to help us find Isaiah Leaf. Clearly, Otto Loring knows Isaiah Leaf; he obviously hates Isaiah Leaf for some reason; and he's motivated to find Isaiah Leaf. He moves in circles that the FBI does not have access to; he can talk to people that the FBI cannot talk to; he could go to Europe and find out where Isaiah Leaf has fled to. What I would like to do is to go visit Otto Loring, and offer to release him from the hospital and from police custody; offer to absolve him of these charges against him here in Panama, on the condition that he go back to Europe, find Isaiah Leaf, and tell the FBI where Isaiah Leaf is hiding."

Jorge Manuel frowned and looked confused. "But this man is going to be released anyway. The charges are going to be dropped."

Dan turned to Jorge Manuel and answered before Agent Williams could speak: "Yes, but Otto Loring doesn't know that. Agent Williams is proposing that we lie to him, to make Otto Loring think he's getting a sweet deal, in order to flush Isaiah Leaf out of hiding."

"Exactly," beamed Agent Williams. "It doesn't cost the FBI anything. We have nothing to lose and everything to gain."

"Well, let me ask you this," Dan said. "Suppose your plan succeeds, and Otto Loring is able to find Isaiah Leaf, and he tells you where Isaiah Leaf is living... what then? You can't arrest him. There's no international warrant for him. What will you do if you find him?"

Agent Williams paused for a moment, as if didn't want to answer that question. "Well, um, yes, we've run into this problem in other cases. Let's just say that we have ways of luring people back to jurisdictions where we *can* arrest them. But our first problem is that we have to find Isaiah Leaf. Then we can figure out how to arrest him."

Dan nodded his head slowly. He was weighing his options. He didn't particularly like Agent Williams, and he wasn't a big fan of helping the FBI, but on the other hand, he didn't have a dog in this fight one way or the other. He didn't care what happened to Otto Loring or Isaiah Leaf or Mark Handel. But he thought about Melissa Leaf, about how beautiful she was. It would be a shame to put that beautiful body in prison, but… on the other hand, she might be an accomplice to a murder—there *was* that little fact. Dan looked over at don Fernando. He could tell that don Fernando wanted to help Agent Williams. There was no telling what other grants Agent Williams could facilitate for the Villa Rosario police department.

Finally, Dan asked, "So what exactly do you want us to do?"

"I would like to go to the hospital and have a little *come-to-Jesus* talk with Otto Loring," Agent Williams said, "but I need to have you all come with me. I think a show of force is important. I can do all the talking, but I need you to back me up if he has any questions."

"I think we can do that," Dan replied.

And so it was that the very next morning, Otto Loring looked up from the hospital bed that he was shackled to, and saw four men walk in, two of them in full Panamanian police uniforms. Don Fernando, Jorge Manuel, and Dan stood beside Agent Williams, and all four men just glared at Otto.

Otto Loring had had many experiences with police officers, and none of them were ever good, so it was natural that he involuntarily pushed himself back into the bed when he saw the four men, as if he was trying to bury himself into the mattress.

"What's going on?" he blurted out.

Agent Williams stepped forward from the group and said, "Oh, we're just here to conduct a little business, Otto." He smiled a sinister smile and pulled out his FBI identification badge from the inside pocket of his jacket and held it up for Otto to see. "I'm agent Ian Williams from the United States Federal Bureau of Investigation, and these other three gentlemen are with the Panamanian police, and they have warrants for your arrest."

Otto's eyes widened. "I—I haven't done anything!" he stammered.

Agent Williams slid his ID badge back into his pocket. "I won't mince words here, Otto. We've got you completely jammed up, and we can put you away in a Panamanian prison for a long, long time. And I guarantee that Panamanian prisons are not like the German prisons you're used to. They're not clean; they're not comfortable; and for a scrawny little bitch like you, they are not safe. The prisons down here are run by gangs. You will not survive. You will be raped, and you will be beaten... beaten every day, beaten the same way you beat up Mark Handel. You do remember attacking Mark Handel in La Chorrera the month before last, don't you? Our witnesses certainly remember you. They all identified you. First degree assault against a tourist carries a minimum of eight years in prison down here. And then there's the attempted burglary of Isaiah Leaf's apartment. We can add another two years in prison for that. And if that wasn't bad enough, you pulled a knife on a police officer and tried to stab him. Attempted murder, Otto. That carries a minimum of twenty years here... twenty years *consecutive* to any other charges. Nah, you're toast, Otto, just toast.

Agent Williams paused for a minute to let his words sink in. Otto was clearly in a panic, looking back and forth at all four men.

"But Otto, I'm in a good mood today, and I might be in a position to help you, assuming, that is, that you cooperate. For some reason, you have a personal grudge against Isaiah Leaf..."

"That motherfucker stole my code!" Otto yelled out.

"I don't care if he stole your dick, Otto," Agent Williams retorted, "*but*... what if there was a way that *he* could do your prison time instead of you? Would that interest you?"

Otto Loring looked at Agent Williams warily. Dan could see the wheels begin to turn in Otto Loring's brain. Otto nodded slowly.

"We have warrants out for Isaiah Leaf," Agent Williams explained, "but he has fled to Europe. He may have changed the way he looks; he's probably using a different name. But he's still traveling in the same circles. He has to maintain his old associates because he's still churning out porn, and he has to keep his business going. And *you* move in the same circles; *you* know his associates; *you* distribute porn through the same contacts... *you* could locate Isaiah Leaf..."

Agent Williams paused again, then said, "Here's the deal, Otto. You can go to a Panama prison for thirty years or you can go to Europe and find Isaiah Leaf."

Agent Williams reached into his side jacket pocket and pulled out a black ankle bracelet. "This is an international GPS ankle bracelet, Otto. We're going to put this on you. It will track you anywhere in the world. We will know where you are at all times. The band is made of steel and Kevlar. You can't cut it off, and if you try to remove it, it sends off an alarm to us, and we will come and arrest you and bring you back to Panama. But if you find Isaiah Leaf, if you can deliver him to us, then we will remove the ankle bracelet, and you can stay in Europe, and we will forget about all these charges here in Panama. But there's a catch, Otto. You only have thirty days. If you don't find Isaiah Leaf in thirty days, we're going to come and arrest *you*, extradite you back here to Panama, and put you in prison."

Agent Williams reached into his inside jacket pocket with his free hand, pulled out a long airline boarding pass, and waved it in front of Otto.

"I have a one-way ticket to Frankfurt, Germany, Otto. It happens to have your name on it. The plane leaves today. I can give you this ticket, or... these fine gentlemen here can serve you with an arrest warrant and take you away to jail. Which will it be?"

Otto's eyes were still wide. He quickly looked at don Fernando's and Jorge Manuel's uniforms. Then, with a shaky hand, he pointed to the ticket in Agent William's hand.

"Good choice, Otto," Agent Williams said snidely. He stepped to the foot of the bed, lifted the hospital sheet off of Otto's feet, and clamped the ankle bracelet onto Otto's ankle. It made a loud solid click. He tossed the boarding pass onto Otto's chest. Then he stood hovering over Otto, reached into his pocket, pulled out a business card, and held that out to Otto.

"I'm going to give you my card. There's a phone number on it. Don't lose this number. It is monitored twenty-four hours a day. We have agents all over Europe, and they can meet you personally within three hours no matter where you are. We know Isaiah Leaf was in Amsterdam six weeks ago. We don't know where he is now, but we do know that he's still producing and distributing pornography in Amsterdam, Germany, and Spain. You find him—you call us. It's that simple."

Agent Williams leaned in close to Otto Loring's face. "Don't fuck this up, Otto, or I'll make sure you spend the rest of your life in prison. Find Isaiah Leaf, by *any means necessary,* you understand?!"

Agent Williams straightened back up. "You'll be released from the hospital this afternoon. Call that number on my card and give us a progress report every three days."

And with that, Agent Williams turned and walked out of the room. Dan, don Fernando, and Jorge Manuel followed him out.

Otto Loring picked up the airplane ticket and the business card and looked at them. His hands began to shake uncontrollably. He couldn't believe his luck.

CHAPTER FOURTEEN

The four men left the hospital and climbed into don Fernando's police car. Agent Williams was feeling proud of himself. He thought that the conversion of Otto Loring into an undercover informant had gone particularly well. On the ride back to Villa Rosario, he bragged to don Fernando about other successful conversions he had made in his career.

"There was this one guy that I managed to turn into a snitch against his own brothers," Agent Williams was saying. "His two brothers were supplying brothels in Tennessee with prostitutes that they brought up from Alabama. Drove 'em right across the state line, which made it a federal crime. Anyway, we caught the youngest brother with about ten ounces of coke. When we arrested him, I arranged for him to spend the night in a jail cell with the biggest, meanest convict I could find. I told the convict he could do whatever he wanted. Made sure the guards didn't disturb them. The next day that little brother was willing to do anything to get out of jail. He ended up testifying against his own family."

Dan sat quiet in the back seat of the car. He cared less and less for Agent Williams. He didn't care for Otto Loring, either. But a part of him regretted helping Agent Williams lie to Otto. Oh, well, Dan thought to himself. It was out of his hands now. Otto Loring would fly to Germany; Agent Williams would fly back to the States; and none of these people would ever come back to Panama. Dan would never have to see any of them again. He was looking forward to resuming his normal retired expat lifestyle in Villa Rosario.

When they got to the police station, don Fernando arranged for coffee and some sandwiches to be brought into the conference room. Agent Williams was continuing to pontificate to don Fernando. Dan watched don Fernando feed Agent Williams open-ended questions and compliments to keep him talking. Dan smiled to himself. Don Fernando was a master at milking the golden cow.

"And this ankle bracelet you put on the suspect," don Fernando asked, "you can follow him anywhere in the world with it? That is amazing technology. I'd love to get some of those. We don't have anything like that down here."

"Oh, no." laughed Agent Williams. "Neither do we. I mean, all ankle monitors use some sort of GPS technology. But it's always just a local bandwidth. There is nothing that can follow someone anywhere in the world. In fact, the ankle bracelet I put on Otto Loring was a dummy. It doesn't transmit at all. It's just plastic. I just told him that story to scare him."

"Really?" said don Fernando. "I am very impressed. *I* believed you!"

Jorge Manuel spoke up. "One thing I don't understand. Señor Landes asked you yesterday: what will you do when you find Isaiah Leaf?"

"Well, we do have agents all over Europe, so we can move very quickly when we locate him," Agent Williams explained. "But *what* we do depends on *where* we catch him. Some countries are more friendly to us than others. In some countries, we can ask that that the local authorities arrest a suspect, and then we can petition for extradition even though we don't have an international warrant. That process can keep a suspect in jail for months. The petition is usually denied, but still, we have interrupted their criminal activity. Other countries are not so cooperative. Sometimes we have to find ways to transport a suspect to another country that is more politically aligned with the US. For example, if Isaiah Leaf has fled to Southeast Asia—someplace like Vietnam, for example. The US has no extradition treaty with Vietnam, but Vietnam has very porous borders, and we could easily relocate him to the Philippines where we don't even need an international warrant to arrest him and ship him back to the US."

Yes, Dan thought to himself, that would be called kidnapping. Agent Williams was certainly committed to getting his man. Back when Dan had worked as a detective in LA, he had known several police officers like Agent Williams. They all were convinced they were doing God's work, helping to bring criminals to justice, helping to rid the world of evil. Many of those officers didn't mind occasionally breaking the law if it meant they could arrest a particularly bad criminal. But Dan knew both sides of that equation. There certainly was too much evil in the world. And every time some police department would arrest a particularly heinous criminal back in the States, there would be a big press conference where some official would announce that they had made the streets safe again. But the streets were never safe again. As soon as one kingpin went down, two more rose up to take his place. Dan was glad he was retired. He no longer wanted any part of that world. As he sipped his coffee, he wondered how much longer he would have to stay in that conference room until he could gracefully exit with some excuse and just go home.

Don Fernando had turned the conversation to drug trafficking. He was quizzing Agent Williams on different types of surveillance equipment. He and Agent Williams were chatting like old friends.

CHAPTER FIFTEEN

Three weeks went by. The rainy season was approaching, and the days in Villa Rosario were turning hot, humid, and cloudy. Dan's life had returned to the type of routine that is eternal and inevitable in tropical countries—a routine that involved strong coffee in the morning, long siestas in the heat of midday, and cold beer in the bars at night. He hadn't forgotten about Isaiah Leaf, his wife Melissa, or that lawyer Mark Handel; rather, he had just put them out of his mind. When you're an expat living in a foreign country, you learn to relegate all visitors to a dusty bin in the corner of your memory. No one ever returns. Even friends from the States who come to visit and swear they'll come back, never return.

Dan also assumed he would never see FBI Agent Ian Williams again. Don Fernando had filled out an FBI application for a grant for surveillance equipment and had sent it to Agent Williams asking for his help, but had heard nothing back. Don Fernando consoled himself with the knowledge that at least his brief friendship with the FBI agent had resulted in a grant to hire a crypto expert.

Jorge Manuel continued to poke around the case. He was able to learn a little more about the late Glen Hartz. It turned out that Glen Hartz was the perfect fall guy to play the role of the dead Isaiah Leaf. He was a solo traveler spending the last of his family's trust fund, still trying to find his life's purpose at age forty-eight. Born decades too late to be a hippie, and too early to be a millennial, Glen Hartz was caught between cultural identities, and lacked the intelligence to develop his own character, and thus, had nowhere to belong. And so, like so many disaffected middle-aged expats with money, he was wandering around Central America looking for paradise. He just happened to bump into Isaiah and Melissa Leaf at an upscale bar in La Chorrera one night. He fit what they were looking for to a T, and they befriended him, charmed him, and made him feel wanted. The bartender remembered the three of them coming in four nights in a row for drinks. Panamanian bartenders always remember gringos who tip well.

Jorge Manuel was able to locate Glen Hartz's next of kin in New Jersey, a step-nephew. The step-nephew notified the trust fund's lawyer who contacted Jorge Manuel and asked for a death certificate. Jorge Manuel called Dr. Javier Hugo. Even though there was no body, no autopsy, and no real identification of the late Glen Hartz, Dr. Hugo was happy to oblige. After all, Jorge Manuel was sending him a lot of business.

And so, life went on as usual, or appeared to be going on as usual. But as fate would have it, things were about to take a weird twist.

It was the middle of the fourth week after that *come-to-Jesus* meeting with Otto Loring in the hospital that don Fernando received a sudden email from Agent Williams. The email was marked "URGENT" and was all in caps. I MUST TALK WITH YOU AND DAN LANDES RIGHT AWAY, the email read. USE THE FOLLOWING ZOOM LINK AT NOON. That sentence was followed by a long website address. Don Fernando had used Zoom before, but it had been a while. He looked at his watch and realized he only had thirty minutes to remember how it worked. He called Dan, and Dan got down to the police station in fifteen minutes.

Don Fernando showed Dan the email and said, "Do you know what this means, Dani?"

"Hmm, it means he has some kind of problem," Dan said.

"Exactly," don Fernando said. "We need to help him, Dani. If we help him, then maybe he will help me get my grant application approved. My department needs new equipment. He wants to do a Zoom conference."

"Okay, well, go ahead and set it up," Dan said.

"I have forgotten how, Dani. Koki put it on my computer last year, but I don't remember how to use it."

"Okay," Dan said. "Let me sit at your desk for a moment. We might need to update the App."

Dan sat down in front of don Fernando's computer, updated the App, and dialed into Agent Williams's Zoom link. Don Fernando pulled up a chair next to Dan and said, "This is exciting. I like Zoom. It is like Star Trek."

After a moment, Agent Williams appeared on the screen. He looked stressed.

There were no introductions. Agent Williams just jumped right into his problem.

"The situation with Otto Loring has gotten out of hand," he said. "I know I told him that he only had a month to find Isaiah Leaf or that I would have him extradited back to Panama, but I was just bluffing... I would have given him more time... but he took me seriously—too seriously! Evidently, he managed to track Isaiah Leaf and his wife all the way to Madrid, Spain, but he couldn't flush Isaiah out. So, I guess he got desperate. He left me a message two days ago saying that he's *kidnapped* Melissa Leaf, and he's holding her captive. He's put word out on the street to all his porn friends that he will only exchange her for Isaiah. This is not good!"

Dan noticed that Agent Williams seemed to be looking directly at him.

"It's one thing to use informants," Agent Williams said, "the FBI uses them all the time. But we can't have our informants kidnapping American citizens in broad daylight. Especially when we don't have an international warrant for Isaiah Leaf! If something happens to Melissa Leaf, and it gets out that I directed Otto Loring to use *any means necessary* to find Isaiah Leaf, then my career is toast!"

Dan nodded, then asked, "Can't you get word to Otto to release her?"

"We've tried that... several times! First, he just said that a deal was a deal. Then we offered to drop the charges against him..."

"The charges that you don't even have," Dan interrupted.

"Right! And he said he didn't believe us. Then we threatened to arrest him for kidnapping, and he said he didn't care, he was going to get even with Isaiah Leaf for stealing his code, and now he's cut off all communication with us."

"And you have no idea where he is?" Dan asked.

"He's on the move. Our Madrid office was able to triangulate his cell phone location, first to a neighborhood called San Isidro. From there we followed him to an area called Chueca, but then we lost the signal. We think he's ditched his cell phone."

Dan nodded. "Yeah, I know that Chueca area. It's pretty sketchy. It would be easy to hide there."

"You know the area?" Agent Williams asked. "Good! That'll come in handy when we get there."

"What are you talking about?" asked Dan.

"I need you to meet me in Madrid," Agent Williams said. There was a tone of desperation in his voice. "You speak Spanish—I don't. You know this Chueca neighborhood—I don't. And most importantly, you know what Melissa Leaf looks like. I've never met her, but police chief Fernando tells me you interviewed her. Plus, you're familiar with the case, and you know what Otto Loring looks like. I need your help, Mr. Landes. The United States needs your help."

Dan felt his face tighten up. He was angry. "It seems to me, Mr. Williams, that *you* created this situation. It was your idea to lie to Otto Loring and to send that psychopath after Isaiah Leaf. There's nothing I can do over in Madrid to help this situation!"

"You can do a lot!" Agent Williams retorted. "You can help me save Melissa Leaf. She's in danger. Plus, I need help navigating Madrid." Agent Williams paused, then lowered his voice. "Look, Dan, I have a budget for what the FBI calls *incidentals*. It's a thousand dollars a day. I'm free to spend that money without having to account for it. I can't officially hire you—there's too much red tape, and I don't have the time for that. Melissa Leaf doesn't have the time for that. But I can pay you one thousand dollars a day for translation services, for assistance, etc., in cash! and I don't have to explain that to anyone. One thousand dollars a day, just to meet me there and help me. What do you say? I need your help, Dan."

Dan crossed his arms and leaned his chair back. He looked over at don Fernando. Don Fernando gave him a pleading look. Dan rubbed his forehead. He did not like Agent Williams. He did not like solving other people's problems. But he did like the idea of free money.

"What about airfare and hotel?" Dan asked.

"I'll cover that." Agent Williams said.

"And does the one thousand a day include travel time?" Dan asked.

Agent Williams swallowed, then said, "Yes."

Dan thought about Melissa Leaf, about those green eyes, that curvy body. It would be a shame if she got hurt due to this FBI agent's blundering efforts to stamp out pornography that hadn't even been produced yet. Plus, Dan thought, if he was going to be paid for travel time, that's a thousand to fly over there, a thousand to fly back, and at least one day there, possibly a few days, just to walk around the Chueca neighborhood... that money would pay for his rent in Villa Rosario for a whole year, maybe two years.

"So," Dan said, "just to be clear: that would be a thousand dollars just to fly over to Madrid, and a thousand dollars just to fly back?"

Agent Williams nodded.

It's not that Dan didn't trust the FBI, but... he didn't trust the FBI.

"I want to be paid each day, in cash," Dan said.

"Not a problem."

"I need to check flights..." Dan started to say.

"I already checked," Agent Williams interrupted. "There's a six o'clock flight this evening from Panama City direct to Madrid on Iberia Airlines. I'll have a ticket waiting for you at the airport."

"Business class," Dan said.

Agent Williams nodded.

Dan shot another look at don Fernando, then said, "Okay, I'll do it."

Agent Williams let out a sigh of relief. "Thanks, Dan. I'll have someone meet you at the Madrid airport."

After Agent Williams hung up from the Zoom call, don Fernando blurted out, "Dani, you were extorting the FBI."

"Nah, amigo, I was just doing a little hardball negotiation. Besides, they're the ones that were extorting me, trying to play on my sympathy for Melissa Leaf. Did you tell them I had interviewed her?"

Don Fernando shrugged apologetically. "Well, yes, of course."

"And did you hint that I thought she was attractive?"

"I may have mentioned that, yes..."

Dan nodded. "Yeah, he acted like he knew that. I think he was counting on that." Dan shrugged. "Oh well, I can use the money. I probably should have asked for more."

"Do you think you can find Otto Loring?" don Fernando asked.

"Not by myself, no. It sounds like he's got other agents over there trying to track Loring down. I'm just going along for the ride because he's scared that this whole thing is going to blow up in his face, and he'll lose his job."

Don Fernando nodded. Dan thought for a moment and then added, "And it *could* blow up. That Loring dude is pretty nuts. He keeps claiming that Isaiah Leaf stole his code. I wish I knew what the truth was behind that... This whole case is pretty nuts... but you know, it occurs to me that Agent Williams is cut from the same cloth as Otto Loring."

"What does that mean, Dani?" don Fernando asked.

"I mean that in some ways, he's just like Otto Loring. He's so determined to get Isaiah Leaf, he'll do anything. He thinks he's got the moral high ground because Isaiah Leaf makes pornography. People like that are dangerous. They create messes."

"But Dani, this Isaiah Leaf is going to be producing child pornography. That is a very bad sin," don Fernando said.

"Yes, I know," Dan said, "but there's always going to be sin. Look at the Garden of Eden. God created paradise, but there was still sin. Sin never stops."

"But Dani... child pornography... you can't let that happen," don Fernando said.

"Yes, yes, I know. Well, I guess I'm going to be doing my part in keeping the world safe," Dan said and smiled. "Well, I'd better get home and pack.

CHAPTER SIXTEEN

Madrid is laid out in very distinct neighborhoods. Its design is a legacy of its medieval history, where each neighborhood was a walled mini-city with its own laws and security forces. You can feel the distinct change as you walk from one neighborhood to another. The streets change in width and direction; the buildings change in size and architecture; and the people change in attitude.

The heart of Madrid is the Puerta del Sol, a huge sun-drenched plaza surrounded by magnificent buildings. The statue of King Charles III on horseback surveys the plaza, and the ten streets emanate from it like spokes from the hub of a wheel.

But walk a few blocks north, across the Gran Via boulevard with its wide sidewalks and fine clothing stores, and you enter the Chueca neighborhood, with its dark narrow twisting streets, brothels, sex shops, and bars. The Chueca neighborhood is Madrid's last refuge of bohemians, artists, prostitutes, and, as fate would have it, one Otto Loring and a very frightened Melissa Leaf.

And thus it was that the next afternoon, after a ten-hour overnight flight from Panama City, a jet-lagged and irritable Dan Landes found himself rendezvousing with Agent Williams in a small café in Madrid. Dan was still wearing the rumpled clothes he had flown over in; Agent Williams was dressed in a suit and tie. Dan was drinking coffee laced with whisky, trying to adjust to the time difference, and listening to Agent Williams drone on about the FBI's local organization of employees and spies.

"Our Madrid office has a full-time staff of over twenty people, plus an additional thirty part-time contractors and consultants. We monitor terrorist activity, immigration issues, anarchist activity, regional uprisings, international chatter, far left activity, far right activity... anything that could in any way affect US interests."

"And yet they can't seem to find one whack job who's kidnapped another whack job's wife," Dan retorted.

Agent Williams glared at Dan, then said, "The FBI has higher priorities in this part of the world."

"Does the local office even know about Otto Loring?" Dan shot back.

Agent Williams stiffened, but then admitted, "Well, no. Only one person knows the whole story. This is an 'off the record' operation."

"Jeez," muttered Dan. "So, you've just got one resource in all of Madrid? How do you expect to find Loring?"

"No, no, no... I've got several people in the Madrid office working on it. They just don't know the details. They think Otto Loring is laundering cryptocurrency for Iran. I've only confided in one trusted agent here regarding the true nature of our operation."

Dan lowered his sunglasses and stared at Agent Williams. "You told the local FBI office that Otto Loring is laundering cryptocurrency for Iran?" he asked slowly.

"Well, I had to tell them something that fell within their domain, so that they would free up resources to help us track him."

"Jesus... you're in deep, buddy," Dan said and pushed his sunglasses back up over his eyes. "And what have your colleagues managed to discover?"

"Well, they narrowed Loring's last cell phone ping to an area of about four-square blocks in the Chueca district," Agent Williams said, pulling out a tourist map of Madrid and unfolding it on the coffee table. Dan could see a small square shaded in red magic marker on the map.

"And when did he use his phone last?" Dan asked.

"Three days ago. It's been dead since then."

"Okay, what else?" Dan asked.

"We have connections with all the banks, of course. We know he used an ATM at this location three days ago." Agent Williams pointed to a small yellow dot on the map, just outside of the red square.

"How much did he withdraw?" Dan asked.

"Six hundred euros."

"Okay, so he's using cash," murmured Dan.

"Additionally, we are monitoring all of Loring's social media accounts: his Facebook page, his Instagram page, his X account, and his messaging apps..."

"But you've got zero hits on those," Dan interrupted, "because he's ditched his phone."

"Right," admitted Agent Williams.

"And he's not using food delivery apps, or else you would have seen credit card activity, right?" asked Dan.

"We've seen no credit card activity," said Agent Williams.

"Okay, what else?"

"We have contacts in the porn world. That's how we found out that he kidnapped Melissa Leaf. He put out word that he has her locked up, and he will only release her if he can meet with Isaiah Leaf."

"How is he supposed to meet with Isaiah Leaf if he's ditched his cell phone?" Dan asked. "How is Isaiah Leaf supposed to contact him?"

Agent Williams pursed his lips and just shook his head. "We don't know," he said.

"Okay. Let's think about this. On his old phone, what was his messaging app of choice?"

"He always contacted me on WhatsApp," Agent Williams said.

"Okay, you need to look at his old phone activity, contact his provider, and see if he used any other messaging app. But for the moment, let's assume that his preferred app is

WhatsApp. If he got a new burner phone, he would probably use a messaging app that he was familiar with, right? So, he'd be using WhatsApp. He would have probably sent out word that Isaiah could contact him on WhatsApp using his new phone number, right? You need to ask WhatsApp for any new accounts created in the last week, with a local phone, that have activity in the Chueca district in the past week... think your local office could handle that?"

"That's actually complicated," Agent Williams said. "We'd have to get new local accounts from all the cell phone providers, and cross-reference those numbers with new WhatsApp accounts, and cross-reference those numbers with cell towers that serve the Chueca district."

Dan nodded his head. "Yup, that's how you'd have to do it. The second thing is that you need to lean on any informants in the porn world. If Loring has sent out word for Isaiah to contact him, that means that every person Loring has told has Loring's new number. You need to find the weakest link in that chain of communication, and get him to give you Loring's new number. This one local FBI person that you've confided in—can you ask him to do that?"

Agent Williams nodded yes.

Dan studied the map again. He looked at the distance from the red square on the map to the ATM location in yellow.

Agent Williams spoke up again. "I looked it up on Google—there are five coffee shops in those four-square blocks. I thought you and I could hang out there and see if we could spot Loring or Melissa."

"That would be a waste of time," Dan said curtly. "He's not taking her for coffee, and he's *not* going out in public unless he has to. But what he *does* have to go out for is food. He has to go to grocery stores or take-out food joints. He's only using cash, and not food delivery apps. So, he either has to buy groceries and cook his own food or pick up food-to-go and pay for it in cash."

Dan thought for a moment, then said. "He didn't impress me as the kind of guy that cooks a lot. He's too impulsive. So I'm guessing that he's relying on take-out food."

Dan pulled out his cell phone and started searching Google Maps for restaurants in the Chueca neighborhood.

"Germans like meat, so we can rule out all the Asian restaurants and the fancy fusion places. He's going to be looking for either a low-key German restaurant that does carry-out, or he's going to look for places that sell some kind of meat dishes to go, like kebab stands."

Dan scrolled though the photos and locations of restaurants that Google suggested were in the Chueca neighborhood.

"Hmm... not many German restaurants in Chueca," Dan said as he swiped through the options. "By the way, suppose we *do* spot Otto Loring... what, exactly, is your plan?"

"Well," Agent Williams responded, "my plan is to confront him and demand he release Melissa Leaf."

Dan snorted involuntarily, shaking his head. "Well, supposing that doesn't work—which it *won't* because he's a psychopath—what's your plan B?"

"Then we'll have to detain him."

"And how exactly are you going to detain him?" Dan asked. "Are you going to pull a gun and say, 'hands up', and hope he complies?"

Agent Williams shrugged and said, "Well, pretty much that, yes."

"And if he laughs and walks away?" Dan asked.

"I *have* a gun," Agent Williams protested. "He can't just walk away."

"You have a gun?" Dan said in disbelief.

Agent Williams reached up with his left hand and pulled the left lapel of his jacket back a few inches. Dan could see a shoulder holster with the butt of a gun.

Dan leaned forward and whispered, "What the fuck, dude? Are you out of your mind? You can't be walking around with a gun in Madrid. That's not legal here. Spain has the toughest gun control laws in the world. Where did you get that?"

Agent Williams looked a tiny bit guilty. "I imposed upon my friend in the local office to loan me one. I figured we would need it."

"Jesus fucking Christ! You need to give it back. You're going to get us both arrested!" Dan said.

"We need firepower," Agent Williams insisted.

Dan was angry. "No, we don't," he hissed. "Look, it's very simple. There's just Otto. He's not working with anyone else. He's holed up somewhere with Melissa, waiting on Isaiah to contact him. He's sneaking out once or twice a day to get food. We don't need a gun. He's kidnapped someone and has imprisoned them—that's a crime! We just need to spot him and then tackle him. There's two of us, and just one of him, and he's a scrawny little jerk. We just need to hold him down and yell for the police. When the police arrive, you show them your badge and tell them about the kidnapping. Let the police rescue Melissa."

Agent Williams pulled back, offended by Dan's insistent tone. "I'd rather not get the local police involved if we can help it," he said. "It raises too many questions. We just need to detain Otto and make him take us back to wherever he's got Melissa Leaf. I've got my contact inside the agency ready to join us at a moment's notice. Then we'll have Otto release Melissa. We'll tell her she's free to go. She'll naturally go running back to Isaiah. I'll have my contact follow her. Once we know where Isaiah is, we'll release Otto."

"And then what? Are you going to arrest Isaiah? You don't have a warrant!"

"I'm working on that," Agent Williams said. "We've got a petition in the Spanish government to grant us extraterritorial jurisdiction to detain Isaiah Leaf on suspicion of manufacturing child pornography."

"Let me get this straight... you're going to release a guy who's committed an actual crime—an actual kidnapping—in order to arrest a different guy on the suspicion that he *might* commit a crime in the future... is that right? I'm not going to let you do that! I agreed to fly over here to help you find Melissa Leaf and keep her from harm. That's *all* we're going to do. We're going to find Otto and we're going to call the police. We're going to let the police release Melissa Leaf. You got that? That's all we're doing. Otherwise, I'm on the next flight back to Panama."

Agent Williams pursed his lips tightly, but then said, "Alright. I need your help."

"Get rid of the gun!" Dan said. "Take it home or give it back to your idiot friend. But get rid of it."

"Alright, alright."

Dan shook his head in disgust, picked up his cell phone, and continued scanning through restaurants in the Chueca neighborhood. Agent Williams just sat sulking.

After a minute, Dan said, "This one looks promising. It's a small take-out stand called Brotzeits. It's got German food to go. It's outside the Chueca area, but it's near that ATM where Otto got his money." Dan pointed to a block on the tourist map. "We'll stake out that place this evening." Dan looked at his watch then said, "It's too early for dinner. I'm going to go back to my hotel and sleep for a couple of hours. You go get rid of that gun. We'll meet back here at five o'clock. We can walk over to that area."

Dan looked at Agent Williams's face. "And go buy a hat," he said. "Something a local would wear, not a tourist hat. And get rid of the suit! I don't know why you FBI guys always wear suits. Go buy a non-descript zip-up jacket. We need to blend in. And for God's sake, get rid of that gun!"

CHAPTER SEVENTEEN

The first evening's surveillance of the Brotzeits food stand proved futile. Dan and Agent Williams took window seats just inside a small café across the street and took turns scanning the area for Otto. The window seats gave them a good view of the food stand across the street. Brotzeits was just a food stand, not a restaurant. There were no indoor tables. Customers could step inside up to a counter and order food. Behind the counter was a large grill and two deep fryers. Two men operated the food stand; both taking orders; both cooking bratwursts, currywursts, doners, and pommes; and both handling the money and bagging up the food to go. The place did good business. But Dan and Agent Williams had no luck. Dan scoured Google Maps for other likely places where Otto might buy food, but he remained convinced that Brotzeits was the most likely place that Otto would go. It was just a question of waiting. While they waited, they nibbled on small orders of tapas. Agent Williams sipped on coffee, and Dan went through several beers.

Dan tried to make small talk with Agent Williams while they waited, but it was like pulling teeth.

"So," Dan asked, "how did you get into FBI work?"

"My father was a cop," Agent Williams said.

"Really? Did he encourage you to join the FBI?"

"Not really, I just always knew I wanted to work in law enforcement," said Agent Williams.

"Interesting," said Dan. "And how long have you worked for the FBI?"

"Ten years," came the terse reply.

"And what do you like most about your work?" Dan asked.

Agent Williams turned away from the window he was gazing through and looked at Dan. "Capturing bad guys," he said, and then turned back to the window. Dan could tell that his questions were irritating the FBI agent.

"Yeah, I supposed you think the world is divided into good and evil," Dan said with a smile, "and that the line that separate the two is very distinct and unmistakable, very black and white."

"Of course," Agent Williams said. "That's why we have laws and courts."

"I used to think that too," Dan said, "back when I was a detective. But now, I have a different view. Now I just see a palette of grays, with some people more gray than others, but everyone just a grimy mixture of various degrees of being unmoored. The more adrift a person is, the more shades of gray I see."

Agent Williams shot Dan a contemptuous look but said nothing. Dan just smiled.

*   *   *

The next evening started off the same way. Dan and Agent Williams resumed their seats at the inside window table of the café across the street from Brotzeits and stared through the window. The two men sat watching silently. Dan had given up on trying to make small talk.

But after about an hour, Agent Williams suddenly blurted out, "There he is!"

The two men watched a small skinny man in a dark overcoat and a low hat walk rapidly up to the entrance of Brotzeits and step inside. Dan squinted. Yes, that was Otto Loring. Dan might have missed him if it hadn't been for Agent Williams. Otto waited his turn at the counter, then ordered some food. He paid and then leaned against the wall and waited while his food was being prepared.

Dan signaled their waiter for the bill. Agent Williams kept his eyes glued to Otto Loring while Dan paid the bill. As soon as Otto Loring got his bag of food and stepped outside of Brotzeits, Agent Williams whispered, "He's moving. Let's go!"

They had to walk briskly to keep up with Otto, but they didn't want to get too close as they didn't want to be spotted. There weren't many people out on the street in this particular neighborhood, so they let him stay about three-quarters of a block ahead. They followed him as he went up two blocks and then left off the main street down a sketchy alley with abandoned buildings. There was no one on this street. Dan and Agent Williams held back at the corner. They watched as Otto entered a narrow doorway in one of the abandoned buildings. As soon as Otto was inside, Agent Williams and Dan sprinted up to the door.

The building was clearly derelict and abandoned. The door that Otto had entered had no door handle or lock.

"You should call for back-up," Dan said.

"No," Agent Williams said breathlessly. "We've got him cornered now. Let's go in."

"That's not a good idea," Dan said.

"Come on!" Agent Williams hissed. He opened the door and stepped into the dark hallway.

"Jesus Christ!" Dan said under his breath and followed him in. The hallway was dark and dirty. Ten feet ahead Dan could see a small staircase that led to a landing with two doors. Agent Williams tread quietly along the hall, with Dan in tow. When they got to the staircase, Dan looked up to the landing. One of the doors had a bit of light that shown from under the door crack. Agent Williams pointed to that door. Then he started stepping slowly up the staircase, taking care to make each step as close to the wall as possible, to avoid making the stairs creak. Dan followed, trying to match Agent Williams's steps.

When they got to the landing, Agent Williams reached inside his jacket and pulled out the same gun that

Dan had insisted he get rid of. Dan's eyes widened. He shook his head no and made an angry face at Agent Williams, but Agent Williams ignored him. Then Agent Williams raised his leg and prepared to kick the door in.

The events that happened next would replay in Dan's mind for many years to come, and in order to understand them, we must return to our opening theme: that everyone has a lucky number. The ancient Greeks believed that the gods had ordained that everyone receive a certain amount of luck in their lives. Some people receive their luck all in one huge event, like winning the lottery, while other people have small, but regular, amounts of luck doled out to them during their lifetimes. Dan certainly had had some lucky breaks in his life, as we all have had, but on this particular day, in this particular abandoned building, on this particular dark and dingy landing, Dan was gifted by the gods with the most fabulous bit of luck of all—the luck of not dying. Dan did not appreciate it at the time. In fact, he barely comprehended it, as the events that followed seem to happen all in a split second, a split second that unfolded in super-slow motion. For as Dan watched in horror, Agent Williams executed a perfect front kick on the old wooden door, and it burst open, sending splinters of wood from the doorjamb flying into the room. The splinters seem to hang suspended in the air. Dan heard Agent Williams shouting something, and the sound of his yell seem to take on a visual mass, flowing through the splinters into the room where Otto Loring was standing, standing with his back to the door but turning, in slow motion, twisting around, with a gun in his hand, and from that gun a white hot flame was slowly emerging, and from that blinding flower of flame a bullet flew out and traveled, spinning, through the air, past the splinters and into the chest of one about-to-be deceased Agent Williams. It was a single clean shot and Agent Williams's body seemed to fold and be jerked back as if pulled by a string, his gun flying out of his hand and falling to the floor. In that microsecond of time, Dan knew that Agent Williams was dead, or about to be dead. Dan also knew that Otto Loring was turning his body, about to move his arm over to aim at Dan. But the gods move in mysterious ways, and sometimes things happen for no apparent reason, no apparent cause, and if those events benefit us, we call it luck. For, as fate would have it, at that exact moment, Otto Loring's gun jammed. Otto would have shot Dan; he intended to shoot Dan. Otto would have shot anyone who intruded in on his world. When you're mad at the world, any target will do. And there Dan was, eyes wide, mouth agape, diving towards the floor for Agent Williams's gun, when Otto pulled the trigger and nothing happened. No flame, no solid sensation of the hammer of the gun hitting the back primer of the bullet still in the chamber. Otto's hand knew something was wrong—there should have been an explosion and recoil, and instinctively Otto started to pull the trigger again. But by this time, Dan had thrown himself to the floor and grabbed Agent Williams's gun and lifted it. The two men pulled their triggers simultaneously, but only the gun in Dan's hand fired.

Dan was sprawled out on the floor about ten feet from where Otto Loring was standing. It's hard not to hit a target that close, and as fate would have it, Dan's single bullet was as accurate and lethal to Otto Loring as Otto Loring's bullet had been to Agent Williams. It's not hard to kill a man if you shoot him in exactly the right spot. Otto Loring's chest caved in around the bullet, as he flew backwards against the wall and slid slowly to the ground.

The sulfuric smell of gunpowder hung in the air. Dan pulled himself to his knees and then to his feet. He looked at the two bodies. Dan knew they both were dead. Each had a crimson stigma on their chest, but the blood was not pumping, not moving. He looked at each of their faces. Dan knew the look of death. He looked down at the gun in his hand. The room was eerily silent. He cocked his head and listened. Did anyone hear the gunfire? Was there the sound of running feet, or someone shouting for the police? He heard nothing.

His old cop brain clicked awake. Anyone who's worked in law enforcement knows how the system works: Once the police arrive, events take on a life of their own, like a strong current that carries you downstream, inquiry by inquiry, to some kind of judgment. Dan didn't want that. How could he answer the inevitable questions? Why was he here in this abandoned building? Why did he have a gun in his hand? Why had he killed someone? What authority did he have to do these things? Why hadn't he called the police in the first place? Who were these other people and how did they all arrive at this same apartment? No, there were way too many questions and not a single good answer.

Dan reached into his back pocket, removed his handkerchief, and carefully wiped the gun in his hand clean. Then, using the handkerchief, he carefully placed the gun in Agent Williams's outstretched hand. Let the police conclude what they might. Let the FBI scramble to defend one of their own, maybe even spin him into a hero, a martyr. Dan had to get out of here. But first he had to find Melissa Leaf.

He stood up from Agent Williams's body which now held the gun. He listened again. He moved as quickly as he could into the interior of the apartment, through a second room. Wait, there was a closed door. He opened it.

Melissa Leaf was on a bed, her hands tied behind her back, her feet bound, her mouth gagged. Dan ran to the bed and began untying her hands, then her feet, and finally the mouth gag.

She started to speak. "No," he said. "Be quiet."

He grabbed her by the arm and lifted her out of the bed to a standing position. She was unsteady on her feet.

"We need to go," Dan said. "Can you walk?"

She nodded yes. She looked a mess, but Dan could see relief in her eyes, relief and questions.

He looked around the room. There was a jacket and a purse on the table. The contents of her purse had been poured out on the table. He went over and scooped the items back into her purse, and then took the jacket and the purse to her and helped her put on her jacket.

"Do you have anything else here? Any other clothes or personal items?" he asked hurriedly.

"No," she managed to whisper.

He grabbed her arm. "Then let's go," he said and guided her out of the room. She stumbled along with him, through the interior room and out to the foyer where the bodies of Otto Loring and Agent Williams lay. Melissa Leaf made an involuntary gasp.

"They killed each other," Dan said. "It's all over. We need to go." He kept his grip on her arm and maneuvered her out the broken door, down the short staircase and out the front door. Dan looked around just before exiting through the door. There was no one on the street.

Melissa's walking was steadier now, but Dan still held onto her arm as they walked.

"Do you know where you are?" Dan asked.

She looked around at the dark buildings and shook her head no.

"Where is Isaiah?"

"We have an apartment near the Museum Reina Sofía," she said.

"Okay," Dan said, "we'll take the metro. I'm going to drop you off near there." Dan stopped and faced Melissa and stared at her as forcefully as he could. "Listen," he said. "You're lucky to be alive. That guy that kidnapped you—that was Otto Loring, the same guy who attacked Mark Handel and who tried to break into your apartment in Panama. He's dead now. He can't hurt you anymore. The other dead man was an FBI agent. They know that Isaiah is planning to sell child porn on the dark web. If he goes through with that plan, eventually, they will catch him. They will catch him and put him in jail, and they will put you in jail. So, make your choice. If he continues to do porn, and if you stay with him, you will end up in jail. Now come on. Let's walk."

As they walked away, Dan could hear the approaching sirens of police cars. He picked up the pace, and they walked quickly, without talking, to a wider street with people, then down another street, and finally to a street near the Chueca metro subway entrance. There were many people pouring in and out of the subway entrance. Dan and Melissa merged into the crowd and walked down the subway stairs.

CHAPTER EIGHTEEN

Don Fernando had been Dan's best friend for almost two decades, so it was natural that Dan wanted to tell don Fernando everything that had happened in Madrid. One of the reasons that the two men were so close was that they shared the same view that what is right and wrong doesn't necessarily always fit nicely into society and law. Even though don Fernando was the chief of police, sworn to uphold the law, both he and Dan had done many things together over the years that would not be considered legal. And thus it was that Dan wanted to share the whole story with don Fernando of how he had killed Otto Loring and placed the gun into Agent Williams's dead hand. Nonetheless, on the flight from Madrid back to Panama, Dan decided not to tell don Fernando those details. He didn't have a reason for not telling him; Dan knew in his heart of hearts that don Fernando would understand completely. At first, Dan told himself that it would just complicate the story. But as he thought about it more, Dan realized that he didn't want to share those details because he was ashamed of what he had done—not for the killing of Otto Loring; after all, that was self-defense. No, Dan was ashamed of himself for getting dragged into the whole mess. He should have refused Agent Williams's offer of a thousand dollars a day. It was a bribe, pure and simple. He had let himself be bribed into helping the FBI agent do something illegal. Dan had no interest in the fate of Otto Loring, nor in the activities of Isaiah and Melissa Leaf. He had let himself be bribed for money... money, and the chance to see Melissa Leaf's green eyes again. He should never have agreed to help Agent Williams. It violated his creed of letting people work out their own fate. He had sold himself for money, and he felt ashamed of that. It was only fitting, he thought, that he never got the full payment for his time. After all, dead men don't pay their debts. Agent Williams had paid for Dan's flight over to Madrid, and for his first few days. But payment for his last day and the flight back to Panama had to come out of Dan's pocket. Dan even had to cough up the final payment to the hotel when he checked out. All in all, he had only broken even on the deal. That's karma, he thought to himself.

And thus it was that two days later, a jetlagged Dan Landes was sitting in don Fernando's office in Villa Rosario, explaining what had happened in Madrid.

"So then, when we got to this abandoned building, I told the FBI agent we should call for reinforcements, but he wouldn't listen. He was so determined to apprehend this Otto Loring guy, don Fernando. He was on a vendetta. So, he went inside the building. I didn't want to follow him, but I didn't know what else to do. If I had stayed outside and had called the police, their arrival would have alert Otto Loring, and that might jeopardize Melissa Leaf... so I went inside, too."

Don Fernando nodded. "That seems reasonable, Dani," he said.

Dan continued. "Then, when we got inside, up a flight of stairs to an apartment where we thought Otto Loring was, this fucking FBI idiot pulls a gun—a *gun*, don Fernando! And he kicks the door in. And there was Otto Loring, just standing there. But then Otto pulls *his* gun and both men immediately started shooting at each other. I guess down deep, both of them must have really hated each other. It all happened in a split second, but they were standing so close they couldn't miss. Before I could move, they had each shot and killed each other. And I ended up standing there in that abandoned building with two dead men."

"That was a lucky break, Dani," don Fernando said. "Then what happened?"

"I searched the apartment and found Melissa Leaf tied up in one of the bedrooms. I untied her, and we got out of there as fast as we could. We took a metro train to the neighborhood where she and Isaiah were staying. Once she recognized where she was, I just let her go."

"You let her go?"

"I let her go."

Don Fernando got up from his desk and went to the sideboard where his coffee maker was. He refilled his coffee cup and then returned to his desk. His brow was furrowed, but his head was nodding.

"I have so many questions, Dani," he said. "To start with, why not call the police after you had freed Melissa Leaf?"

"I didn't need to call them. As we were leaving, I could hear their sirens coming. But I didn't want to stick around. This situation was simply too messy, don Fernando. Most crimes need the police to sort things out, to get to the truth; but some crimes are so messy that adding the police doesn't help at all; it just makes things worse, and the truth never comes out. That FBI agent was acting illegally. He had no warrant for Otto Loring, nor for Melissa or Isaiah Leaf. Yet, he was an FBI agent, working with his FBI office in Madrid to track Otto Loring. That was basically an illegal operation. His plan was to track Otto down and arrest him. He was way outside his jurisdiction. Second, both of those men had guns, which is illegal in Spain. I didn't know the FBI agent was armed, but there I was, trespassing inside a building *with* him. Any Spanish cop would assume I was *helping* the FBI agent, and that I *knew* he had a gun. That would make me part of a conspiracy, which I wasn't. No... this way was simpler. I knew that when they found the bodies, the police would discover that one of the dead men was an FBI agent, and the other one was a lowlife criminal. Then they would contact the US Embassy and the FBI office in Madid, and the FBI office would scramble to protect their agent and say that he was investigating terrorism or something. No one will care about Otto Loring, and everyone will accept that the two men had an unfortunate and violent encounter, and they both died."

Don Fernando nodded and said, "It *is* cleaner this way. But my second question is: what about our murder warrants for the girl and her husband?"

Dan shrugged. "What was I supposed to do, don Fernando? There is no international warrant out for them. If I had gone to the police in Spain, they couldn't have arrested them. Besides, if Isaiah and Melissa Leaf ever wander back to Panama and get arrested, I doubt that the court here could get a conviction. The guy they killed—I forget his name—no one seemed to care that he died. Jorge Manuel said his only next of kin seemed relieved that he was dead; more money for him, you know. We don't even have a body. And that coroner, Dr. Javier Hugo, can you imagine him on the witness stand? He's an idiot. This way, with murder warrants out for them here, they will never come back to Panama."

"True, Dani. So, she is back with her pornography-making husband?"

"I assume she went back to him the day I dropped her off," Dan said. "I don't know if she will stay with him."

"And this Isaiah Leaf is free to do his plan to make child pornography?"

Dan shrugged. "I don't know, don Fernando. I just don't know. I mean, maybe he'll change his mind. I did tell Melissa Leaf that the FBI knew that Isaiah was planning to create child porn—maybe that will scare him into not doing it. But maybe not. I just don't understand why people do what they do."

"But this child pornography is a bad thing, Dani."

"Yes, I know, don Fernando, but people do bad things all the time. That was the FBI agent's mistake. He wanted to arrest Isaiah Leaf *before* he created any child pornography; he wanted to *prevent him* from doing bad things. I don't think that's possible. But to answer your question, I don't know what Isaiah Leaf will do. But if he does persist in his plan and creates CGI child pornography, eventually he'll be arrested. He won't be able to get away with it. He's too well known. He's got an arrest warrant in the States for insurance fraud. He's got an arrest warrant here for murder. He's on the FBI's radar. His world has become a smaller place. For the rest of his life, he'll be looking over his shoulder. That's a horrible way to live."

Dan paused for a moment and reflected. Then he said, "And to think, don Fernando, six months ago, he was king of the world, a millionaire, living with a beautiful wife, able to travel anywhere... and now, he's a fugitive living in Europe... People sure do fuck up their lives."

-fin-

ABOUT THE AUTHOR

Robert Rahula was born in Spain to an American father and Spanish mother but grew up in Virginia on the farm of his paternal grandparents. He returned to Menorca, Spain in the 1960s to pursue his writing career. Over the past thirty years, Robert has published dozens of books of prose and poetry in Spain and in the United States. Readings of his poems appear on his YouTube channel, his Facebook page, and his website robertrahula.com. He travels Europe and Central and South America for several months a year, giving readings and lectures, and spends the rest of his time writing.

www.ingramcontent.com/pod-product-compliance
Lightning Source LLC
Chambersburg PA
CBHW072140300726
48975CB00003B/1137